SUBMARINE ATTACK!

Another explosion, this one even nearer, erupted in the water.

"Make some tracks, Casey. And while you're at it, make it a little harder to draw a bead on us," McKay said. "Then we'll just sit and let them come to us. You about ready on that nineteen, Tom?"

"Loaded and ready," Rogers acknowledged.

Mobile One settled to a level crawl just out of range and right in the middle of the stream. The turret whined as Tom slowly swiveled the M-19 grenade launcher toward its target.

Suddenly the tiny deck of the sub squirmed with activity. McKay watched through the viewpoint as a bearded man dropped the recoilless rifle overboard and scrambled for the open hatch. "They see you coming, Tom," McKay smiled.

"Do they?" Rogers said. "Do you think they'll see this?" He fired the grenade launcher and the baby submarine erupted in a ball of flame . . .

THE  GUARDIANS
SNAKE EYES

RICHARD AUSTIN

JOVE BOOKS, NEW YORK

THE GUARDIANS: SNAKE EYES

A Jove Book / published by arrangement with
the author

PRINTING HISTORY
Jove edition / December 1990

ISBN: 0-515-10407-8

Jove Books are published by The Berkley Publishing Group,
200 Madison Avenue, New York, New York 10016.
The name "JOVE" and the "J" logo
are trademarks belonging to Jove Publications, Inc.

PRINTED IN THE UNITED STATES OF AMERICA

10 9 8 7 6 5 4 3 2 1

To Larry Steelbaugh for the push,
and Bryce Marshall for the tremor,
and both for their friendship and encouragement.

ACKNOWLEDGMENTS

My thanks to Gary "Ratt" Hudson of Sipes' Gun Shop for his expert knowledge of weaponry, and to Terry P. Thodie for his military technical assistance.

PART
ONE

PROLOGUE ——————————————

The easy-running slough bathed Woody's bare feet, and the boy wondered, in that peculiar twelve-year-old way, why the sensation was warm when everybody knew that water was supposed to feel cool. He dangled his slender legs over the side of the minnow dock and twirled his feet in the green water below. He watched the reflection of the moon, which rode full in the southern sky, bob like a silver cork on the tiny waves. He drew the early spring air deeply into his lungs, inhaling the sweet smells that seemed to flow downstream with the water. It was his favorite time of evening, just after dusk, when the lightning bugs flared like sparks from some ancient fire, and the deep pin-oak woods lining the banks came alive with the sounds of the night.

He had his overalls rolled up, just like Momma said, so his britches' legs wouldn't get wet and give him a cold in the still-cool air. He thought that was dumb, but he did it anyway just to please his mother. Not that Rachel would know. By this time she would already be in a drugged-out stupor with the rest of the grown-ups down on the old steamboat that served as the community headquarters just around the bend. He could hear the muffled strains of their music, either the Grateful Dead or The Band, he wasn't quite sure. All that old-fart music sounded alike to him.

He preferred to dwell on the sights and sounds of his world—the night sky over Indian Bay. He lay back on the dock and aimed his imagination at the sea of stars that sailed overhead. There was Mars, the planet of blood, just above the horizon, and beyond that, the inhabitants of the Milky Way all swirling and twinkling against the dark canopy that shrouded the earth. He spotted Venus, the evening star, fixed cold and low beyond the dark line of the trees. Then the constellations jumped into focus—Orion's hourglass, Leo high up, and Virgo to the east. He knew these from the encyclopedias the Ralstons provided for him. He just wished he had a good set of binoculars, or better still, a telescope, with which to spy on the heavens. *What mysteries lurked beyond the atmosphere?* he wondered. *What worlds floated out there? What creatures lived and died not knowing or caring of earth's existence?*

Then Woody blinked at the flash. It came suddenly, just to the right of the star Capella, descending in the northwest. A shooting star, he supposed. Just what he was waiting for. But it continued its flare longer than any the boy had seen in the past. It must be a comet, he concluded, though he knew of no comet approaching earth at this time that would be visible in the northern hemisphere. *Perhaps it was a phenomenon of the One Day War,* he thought. *Maybe we blew the planet slightly off its axis and so invited a whole new cluster of comets to visit the world. No, we would probably all be dead by now if that had happened.* Or so the encyclopedia had told him. Still, it was odd.

The flash continued, and instead of dimming, it grew increasingly brighter—and larger. *What the hell is going on?* Woody wondered as the glowing object grew. Then a cloud of light fired from the object at an angle and trailed off on a separate course. Woody twitched at the sight and sat up. The smaller tail sparked off over the horizon, dying as it fell. But the main body got bigger and brighter as it approached. It looked close enough to touch—larger than all the stars and even the planets in the sky. Then it changed shape from a bright disc with a tail to a pulsating oblong of fire. *It must be a meteor entering the earth's atmosphere*, he thought. It was his own private shooting star blazing toward him, burning from the heat of the friction generated by the very air he breathed.

Though the object was hurtling down at him at an incredible rate, he could discern that its speed had subtly decreased. And, as it slowed, the meteor, or whatever it was, changed shape. It grew shorter and seemed to pulsate less. Then Woody realized that the thing was cooling as it slowed and so was extinguishing its own fire. It would soon burn out and lose its tail and vanish in the sky as suddenly as it had appeared. The boy stood transfixed as he watched the tail shorten, and indeed disappear, and the throbbing flare subside. Finally, it shrank to a small glowing disc high in the night. Woody knew that any second he would lose sight of even that faint gleam, and his meteor would fall somewhere to earth, nothing more than a smoking rock from outer space. The thought saddened him, so he strained to hold the glimmer in his gaze to the last perishing moment. And that moment came while the object hovered above the moon. The boy saw it flicker once then disappear. He just stood there, head thrown back, peering at the spot where his meteor had died.

Then a blur suddenly appeared over the face of the moon. It was a dark bead, really, that seemed to waft there in suspension, backlit by lunar light. Then three larger dots appeared above the original and they all seemed connected. Woody watched, stunned, as the odd triangle swung there, like a celestial pendulum, against the fat face of the moon. It was for just an instant that the boy's sharp young eyes held this phenomenon before it floated below the moon, but for Woody it was a protracted year of glory. In all of the nights he had stood guard since the accompanying boredom had turned him toward the stars, he had never seen anything like the wondrous sight he beheld tonight. He conjectured for a moment that Copernicus must have felt the same way upon his discovery of the solar system.

Still staring at the moon, he blinked twice, giving himself a visual nudge just to make sure he had seen what he thought he had seen. His mother had often accused him of making things up just to tease her, but this was no product of an overactive imagination. Whatever Woody had seen, it had been for real.

His eyes hurt from the strain, and he started to turn away. But just as he moved he thought he saw a another faint twinkle in the sky. He swiveled back and dropped his gaze several inches below the moon. And there, just as surely as he was standing on a dock on Indian Bay, was a set of red and green blinks firing off simultaneously at intervals. They couldn't be anything else but a set of running lights, identification beacons on an aircraft. Maybe it was just an airplane that had sneaked under his stare while he was preoccupied with the show on the moon. But if it was a plane, why were its lights drifting straight down instead of gliding horizontally? And why was there no sound though the lights, judging by their size, were so close—certainly close enough for him to hear the thunder of any accompanying engines?

When the realization finally hit him, the boy let out a whoop like some sort of demented crane. What he saw was a craft, all right, but it was no mere airplane. It was the very thing he had watched enter the atmosphere: a machine from outer space, perhaps even from another planet—it dangled there, suspended from three huge parachutes, as if it were pasted against the moonlit sky. And all Woody could do was stand paralyzed and watch it float straight toward Indian Bay—and him.

CHAPTER
ONE ──────────────────────

Dr. John Mallory winced as he reached for the control panel with his right hand. His groan interrupted the cool, dispassionate tone of "Londonderry Air," a tune the physicist whistled to control his panic. The pain stabbed his shoulder like a hot blade, and for an instant he doubled over in the command chair of the escape pod, ignoring the visual and audio cacophony of the control panel that blazed before him. The digital instruments flashed glaring red warnings, and an obnoxious alarm screamed throughout the tiny cabin.

"Turn that infernal thing off!" Mallory shouted. "I already know it's trouble we're in." The anger in his voice seemed to accentuate his County Cork lilt.

The black-clad figure to his right raised a gloved hand to a toggle above his head, and the screeching instantly ceased.

"Remind me to be giving you thanks, Jonesy, if speech is something I can still manage after this thing is over," Mallory said. His long upper lip slid into a greasy smile, brightening his pink face against the flash of premature white that surrounded his head like a neon halo. The sick smile, the florrid face, the wild, white hair splaying from under his headset, and the blood saturating his shoulder, combined to give Mallory the appearance of a latter-day Andy Warhol watching a gang rape.

Mallory knew he had good reason to look flustered. He and Jones were approaching Earth's atmosphere in a capsule whose heat shield was either slightly damaged or totally useless. Though the sophisticated instrumentation told him there was a problem with the shield, it did not tell him to what extent. But no matter. In a few seconds, when the friction of the re-entry raised the temperature of the nose cone to 3,000 degrees Fahrenheit, he would know all too well.

Mallory chuckled at the irony. Though the contemplation of leaving this life in the form of a human torch did not amuse him, he nonetheless realized he was lucky to still be alive at all. Except for Jones, all of his colleagues were now dead—blown into tiny pieces destined to float as extraterrestrial specks through an eternal universe. Had it not been for Jones, who cleverly eluded the American devils to secure the escape pod and then carried Mallory aboard, fending off Drs. Sejnowski and Mitchell for the last remaining seat, Mallory would now be no more than so many particles of space dust orbiting the earth. After ejecting from the Cygnus platform, Jones even managed to bandage the doctor's shoulder, keeping Mallory from bleeding to death, at least for a while. Of course, Mallory knew that Jones had to save him because the Englishman didn't know the proper sequence for re-entry. *Once again*, Mallory snickered, *there is no substitute for intelligence*.

Indeed, it was Mallory's cleverness that foresaw the need for an escape pod at the outset. After all, he had heard the reputation of the Guardians, that elite team of American troubleshooters, who, since the One Day War, had continuously eluded and frustrated the sadistic aims of Yevgeny Maximov, chairman of the Federated States of Europe and Mallory's current employer. The moment he heard he was going into space to blast American targets, Mallory knew the Guardians would find a way to reach orbit. What he didn't know was that they would prove to be as cruel as his Ukrainian captor. Especially that McKay—Lt. William McKay—who left him bleeding and in pain to die aboard the space platform.

"McKay," Mallory vowed out loud, "if I survive this, then, by the angels, I will see you gutted like the animal you are!"

The gunshot wound sent needles of searing pain shooting through his shoulder and reminded Mallory of Sylvie Braestrop, the stupid bitch who had shot him. It wasn't bad enough that she planted a .38-caliber bullet in his body. No, she had to override his reprogramming of the auto destruct function of the on-board computer, which effectively assured the destruction of Cygnus X-1 along with all of the priceless programming equipment designed specifically to run the laser cannon—the weapon with which Maximov had planned to rule the planet. And while she was accomplishing this, she added insult to injury by continuously proclaiming her love for him. *The silly trollop*. He could hear her now—*"We will die together, John."* What insipid *horseshit*, he thought. *As it turns out, though, dear Sylvie, you are basking in God's glory without me. At least for a while*. He knew, however, that if he did survive, he would one day lament the loss of those great tits.

"We're entering the bloody Chemosphere, doctor!" Jones's tone indicated he was approaching panic at warp speed. Plus, his British accent was already beginning to grate on Mallory. After all, a young officer with the same accent had shot down his grandfather in the streets of Belfast thirty years before.

But first things first. Right now Mallory had to deal with some tricky telemetry problems. Specifically he had to choose the precise angle to position the space pod for re-entry into the atmosphere. And for this he needed to know the exact extent of damage to the craft's heat shield. But all he knew for certain was that moments after he and Jones had launched safely away from Cygnus X-1, the platform had exploded into thousands of pieces of space shrapnel, and one had fragged the heat shield. There were no external video units with which to review the damage and, even if there had been time, no space suits for a firsthand look. There was a single viewport, but its position precluded a view of the nose. This left Mallory with but two remaining resources: his innate genius for physics and his inherited luck of the Irish.

"Chemosphere re-entry confirmed." Mallory whispered his acknowledgment through the microphone of his headset. He understood the need to project a calmness to counteract Jones's near-hysteria. They were, after all, hurtling toward Earth, just 160 miles below. And, in less than a minute, they would descend to an altitude of 115 miles and enter the third level of ionization, a position after which they could no longer effectively use their instruments. At 75 miles they would, for an instant, be able to see the Aurora Borealis, the great Northern Lights, just before the friction from the earth's atmosphere transformed their helpless pod into a chunk of pure flame.

Mallory wondered what would become of Emily after his death—sweet Emily, his eleven-year-old daughter and the light of his life. If Maximov's goons hadn't captured her in their Geneva flat, then Mallory wouldn't be in this hellish predicament in the first place. Of course, he already would be dead, if his judgment of Maximov held true. For he never would have performed those despicable deeds—raining death upon the planet from orbit—had Maximov not held Emily hostage. But that was beside the point. What mattered now was what Maximov would do to his daughter. At least while alive Mallory could pretend to do Maximov's twisted bidding and so offer Emily a modicum of protection. But dead, Mallory could only hope that the object of Maximov's depravity was limited to girls beyond the age of eleven—a notion which he felt sure was purely wishful thinking.

"Doctor, I've picked up something on the scope!" Jones's excitement jolted Mallory out of his reverie.

"What is it?"

"I don't know."

"Well, what do you think it is?" *These fucking Englishmen have no imagination at all,* Mallory reminded himself.

"I can't make it out," Jones replied, flustered. "It just suddenly appeared in front of us."

In front of us? Mallory thought. *This could be a stroke of good fortune.* "How big is it? Never mind. Let me see."

Mallory shoved Jones out of the way and positioned himself directly in front of the scope. There, just ahead and directly in their path, an unmistakable green blip dotted the black background of the screen.

As best he could discern from the radar, the object was not as big as the escape pod.

"Damn! It's too small."

"Too small, sir?"

"Yes, you incredible dolt. It's too small to use as a shield."

Jones frowned and scratched the top of his head. Then he beamed. "Oh yes, sir. I see now."

Mallory rolled his eyes toward the ceiling, then focused again on the scope. He punched an entry into the keyboard of the craft's computer, and a graphic model of the object's shape along with clumps of numerals appeared on a terminal screen. The data confirmed Mallory's suspicions.

The object's dimensions were definitely not large enough to form an effective heat shield for the escape pod. However, its peculiar shape caught Mallory's attention. The computer model displayed something that looked oddly like a combination of a dog's hind leg and a scorpion's tail. *Could it be,* Mallory thought, *that it survived the explosion? Impossible.* "Yet, could it be?"

"Could what be, sir?" Jones asked.

"What? Oh, nothing, Jonesy. Never mind." But Mallory wondered still.

"Doctor, we're approaching the third level of ionization. What should we do?"

"For the love of *Jaysus,* let me think!" Mallory barked, his Gaelic roots flaring.

"But, Doctor, once we penetrate the third level we can no longer depend on our instruments."

"Thank you so much for reminding me. Now kindly be silent!"

Mallory studied the screen closely. The object's boomeranglike shape intrigued the physicist in him, and he wondered if placing the pod directly behind the crooked joint just off the debris's center would do the trick. The maneuver would utilize the object's maximum shield dimensions, after all, and, if Mallory's guess was correct, its titanium structure just might withstand the incredible temperatures generated by the friction of the re-entry. It was certainly worth a try. It might even work. Besides, he had no other ideas and he was fresh out of time.

"Prepare the attitude jets!" Mallory snapped.

Jones lurched forward, flipping switches and pushing buttons with a fury. "Attitude jets ready, sir," Jones said. "We're entering the third level now."

"Forward starboard jet. Five seconds. Ready? Fire!"

"Ahead starboard, five, sir."

Mallory felt the smooth adjustment as he watched the results on the scope.

"Port ahead three."

Jones repeated the command as it was executed, then looked over Mallory's shoulder at the scope. The pod corrected to a position that settled just behind the inner elbow of the space object.

"Reverse starboard and port, one second," Mallory commanded.

The pod nestled into the vortex formed by the object's legs.

"We're there, sir," Jones chirped. "Perfect position under the circumstances."

"Thank you, Jonesy. Now what's our altitude?"

"Approaching eighty miles, sir. Re-entry twenty-six thousand feet below."

Mallory checked the tautness of his seat harness and tugged at the clasps. They held firm. He looked to his left and noticed Jones emulating him. It would only be a matter of seconds now.

Suddenly thousands of brilliant lights showed through the ship's viewport. Both men watched the Aurora Borealis with mixed emotions for they knew that the dazzling display also signaled the edge of the earth's atmosphere.

"Hang on, Jonesy. Here we go!"

"Good luck, sir."

The Northern Lights disappeared behind a sheet of flame as the pod followed it's impromptu shield into the wall of the earth's atmosphere. A vibration grew into a quake which shook the machine like a laboratory mixer. Mallory glanced over at Jones and saw a blur that faintly resembled a human being.

Then the physicist began to notice the effects of the gravity forces. At three Gs he felt as if his neck were growing; at four Gs he wondered if his upper jaw might possibly have entered the lower part of his brain; and at five Gs he thought the top of his head had come off.

The temperature rose in the cabin as the heat buildup from the re-entry process covered the exterior of the pod in a blanket of fire. Mallory gasped for air as he fought through his own perspiration to focus on the blurred instruments before him. He didn't know the cabin temperature because the heat gauges for the entire ship were placed before Jones. And communicating, even through a headset, was impossible at five Gs. Also, the chances that Jones could even read the instruments were slim and none. Mallory looked over again at his copilot and saw a head locked in a violent tremor and fronted with skin stretched into a grotesque distortion of a face. Oddly he thought that Jones's face fit the Englishman perfectly, and he wondered for a moment if he, too, wore a mask of sublime stupidity.

Mallory had little concept of where they were and no idea at all where they would land if they indeed survived this nightmare. All thoughts of proper telemetry were shunted upon the decision to follow the space debris on its dive toward the earth. He knew only that the atmospheric wall began about seventy-five miles from earth and that the Aurora Borealis disappeared at sixty miles altitude. But all he could see through the tempered porthole was a raging inferno that must surely consume their substitute shield in a matter of seconds. If only he had some information upon which to act. If only he could *do* something.

The computer model had strongly suggested that the space debris upon which they were gambling their lives was actually a piece of the Cygnus X-1 platform—specifically a robotic arm that operated outside the station—and was apparently ejected intact into space when the orbital vehicle exploded. If this guess was correct, then the arm might just withstand the heat of re-entry. Mallory knew it was constructed of titanium, whose melting point, if his undergraduate chemistry still served, was 3,035 degrees Fahrenheit, or just 35 degrees more than the nose-cone temperatures generated during the hottest point of re-entry. So, if the arm did not brake up from the turbulence, or did not tumble too drastically, then the escape pod that followed just might have a chance.

The roar from the turbulence and the ablative effect of the plasma stream that flamed over the pod rose to an unnerving crescendo, and Mallory felt himself dangerously close to screaming. Then came new sounds—noises loud enough to be heard even over the din in the cockpit. A distinct crack, like an explosion, followed by a hideous human wail, pierced Mallory's brain. For an instant he thought he had heard his own scream, his own howl of pain. But he felt nothing other than the surging dread that perhaps the ship had finally broken apart. He looked to his left to check Jones's reaction to the noises. What he saw there convinced Mallory that this time the scream he heard was definitely his own.

He shrieked hysterically as he watched Jones's headless body jerk and twitch in the control chair next to him. A quivering slab of crimson formed above Jones's neck, his heart relentlessly pumping blood out through the severed stump. His trunk lurched, and his arms flailed about as if he were trying to retrieve his missing head. One mindless hand slapped Mallory in the face, and the physicist recoiled in horror, screaming. The floating pool of blood stretched and clumped about the cabin like the contents of a lava lamp suddenly freed in semiweightlessness.

Mallory fought to gain control of himself. His involuntary wailing finally subsided into periodic sobs which shuddered through his terrified system. When he was able to think he turned his attention to the control panel and noticed that much of it in front of Jones was blown away. He could only surmise that the special glass that had covered many of the instruments had sliced through Jones's neck during the explosion, evidently the loud crack he had heard. Perhaps the line that held the control panel coolant had ruptured, or perhaps an electrical spark had set off one of the exotic gasses housing the instruments—Mallory didn't know. And at this point he didn't care. All he knew was that Jonesy, one of the few humans he had ever liked, was dead. And all because of McKay!

Mallory was too preoccupied with his own terror to notice that the temperature in the cabin had lowered rapidly. He glanced up at the viewport, however, and was relieved to see that the wall of flame, which had accompanied the pod throughout its plunge, had disappeared. In its place rode the moon, shimmering full beyond the glass. A violent jerk pushed him against his seat harness, and the straps cut into his chest. Two more jerks, smaller, followed, and Mallory noticed the pressure of normal gravity for the first time in weeks. He smiled to himself as he lay back and watched the three giant parachutes, silhouetted against the moon, float beyond the porthole, gently braking his fall to earth.

"Home," he shouted out loud. "By God, I've made it!"

Then he felt something odd—something wet and heavy pushing against his crotch. With a mixture of curiosity and dread, Mallory peered slowly down. And there, perched upright in his lap and wearing its customary look of idiotic surprise, was Jones's severed head.

It was Mallory's last image from space before he screamed once and passed out.

CHAPTER TWO

"Shit." McKay moaned as he groped his way into consciousness. "This is getting to be a habit." Through a steadily adjusting blur, he scanned the interior of the space shuttle StarVan. About all he could tell was that the orbiter was at rest, still in one piece, and deathly quiet.

It was the second time within the hour that Lieutenant William McKay had awoken from an artificially induced nap. The first came at 125 miles altitude when a piece of space debris from the exploding Cygnus X-1 platform knocked out the port engine and most of the attitude jets aboard StarVan, sending the marine into a bulkhead. The second came at zero altitude when the crippled minishuttle crash-landed somewhere in Alaska.

At least this time *he* didn't run into anything, McKay reasoned as he cradled his throbbing head. He checked his seat harness, which was still firmly intact. He looked around to see if he could determine what had hit him, but the StarVan was littered with weapons and equipment that the crew hadn't had time to secure before the rushed re-entry. It could have been anything.

McKay waited a moment for his focus to improve but then grew impatient. *So what if I puke and fall down*, he thought, ripping at his seat belts. He had to check on the rest of the Guardians. He swung his legs over the side of the contoured launch chair and thought about standing up. Then he eased to his feet and braced for the inevitable wave of dizziness and nausea to sweep over him. He noticed his vision had improved, but he still could not focus properly. Suddenly his head felt as if it had just been injected with a liter of pure helium while a column of bile marched up his throat. He bent over, supporting himself on his knees, and fought the queasiness.

"God," he said out loud, gulping for air.

"Yes?" came a female voice from behind him and just to the right. "What can I do for you, my son?"

McKay painfully panned toward the tail section. And there, buried under a pile of equipment, lay Antoinette Lee.

"Christ. There for a minute I thought I'd survived," McKay groaned. "But now I know I'm dead, and this is hell."

"Quit your bitchin' and get this shit off me." Lee's voice sounded like a chain saw cutting through concrete, and McKay wondered how such a small woman could have such a big mouth. "My fucking arm is broken, you know."

McKay remembered that he and Tony were the last to enter StarVan after the orbital combat and that she indeed had broken her arm when Cygnus exploded.

"Aww, has baby got a boo boo on her arm?" McKay couldn't resist.

"Kiss my ass!" Tony brayed.

"Oooh, I just might take you up on that someday," McKay oozed. "But, I'd have to gag you first."

"Is that how you like your women, McKay? Bound and gagged?"

Like everything else, McKay preferred his sex straight,

but this new idea was worth considering. For a moment he envisioned a naked Tony, handcuffed, hooded, and draped over a banister with her lovely Asian ass floating in the helpless position.

"Yeah, a good grudge fuck is just what you need!"

"Someday, McKay, I'm going to brake your goddamn jaw."

"A little foreplay, huh? That's kinky."

"Get this shit off of me!"

"Anything you say, dear." McKay chuckled to himself as he staggered aft, knowing he had won the round.

He uncovered Tony carefully, not that he was worried about her arm, but he was afraid she might try to kick him. This little Chinese-American broad was 165 centimeters of pure wildcat. And the fact that she had achieved the rank of lieutenant commander in the U.S. Navy hadn't tamed her any. The call sign emblazoned on her F-18 was *Renegade*, after all. She was almost the first official female fighter jock in any branch of the services, then almost the first female shuttle commander and pilot, but the One Day War had changed all that.

It hadn't, however, changed her ability in the cockpit. McKay had watched her flame two F-5s and two F-4Es above Vandenberg Air Force Base before she was wounded and forced to bail into the California sky. He had gained a mountain of respect for the cute but mouthy little chink that day. He just wished that all the women he ran into weren't so goddamn butch.

"How's everybody else?" Tony asked.

"Don't know yet. I've been baby-sitting." McKay slipped his arm around Tony's tiny waist, and together they snaked their way through the trashed-out fuselage. Up near the nose they heard a sound—an "uuuggghh" that came from the pilot's chair. Then:

"Anybody got a wine cooler?" The accent was pure California surfer.

"I guess that means Casey's OK," McKay smiled.

"What hit me?"

"Nothing much," Tony quipped, "just the entire contents of the ship." She leaned over to unbuckle Lieutenant Kenneth "Casey" Wilson's harness and noticed his face was bleeding. "You won't be doing any shaving commercials for a while—ouch!" She winced when she tried to use her arm.

"Here, let me do that," McKay intervened. He loosened Casey and helped the Air Force pilot to his feet. With difficulty Tony opened a first aid kit and offered a bandage.

"You got a union card for that kind of work, lady?" It was Tom Rogers, who appeared out of nowhere. As the team's medical specialist, Lieutenant Rogers relieved Tony of the kit and went to work on Casey's face. "I'll check your arm as soon as I stop the bleeding here."

Tony gave Rogers a blank stare then glanced quizzically at McKay. Her look asked, Where the hell did he come from? McKay just shrugged and continued searching through the cabin. The marine officer was long since used to Rogers's ability to bend the rules of metaphysics. He knew that the Special Forces training was what did the trick, and Rogers took to that green beret mumbo jumbo like a mystic to the moon.

"I guess there's no point in looking at your head, Billy," Rogers deadpanned. "But whatever hit it could probably use surgery." Tony let out a single sharp laugh, like a bark.

"I love you, too, Tom." McKay smirked.

"Before you two kiss, could one of you please get me out of here?" The voice was muffled, as if it were coming from behind a wall.

"Where are you?" McKay shouted.

"Here! Behind the hatch."

Rogers never looked up from his task. McKay and Tony scanned the cabin, which was filled with hatches, then looked at each other blankly.

"In the head, dammit!" came the disembodied voice.

McKay chuckled as he waded toward the ship's privy. "We didn't catch you with your pants down, did we?"

"Any assistance you might offer unaccompanied by lame witticisms would be greatly appreciated."

McKay laughed out loud. Even in the most compromising positions Lt. Comdr. Sam Sloan could always be counted upon to maintain a courtly manner. It was the Southern gentleman in him.

McKay opened the door, then lurched backward as if shot by a twelve gauge.

"Ooooh weee! Pheeew!" McKay's grimace started at his nose and worked through his entire body. "You smell like . . . well . . . like shit!"

"You have an enormous talent for the obvious, Billy. Now give me a hand."

"You ain't gettin' no part of my body in there." Revulsion had stretched McKay's face into an elastic caricature of itself. "You're on your own on this one, pal."

"I think you'd better get him out of there, McKay." Tony shot the remark over her shoulder as she opened the main hatch, and Rogers helped Casey through it. "I smell fuel!"

"You wouldn't let me fry in this shit, now would you, ole buddy?"

McKay thought Sloan's choice of words was appropriate as he looked around the fuselage for something to grab. He settled on a Franchi autoloading combat shotgun, the longest thing he could find, and handed it barrel-first through the hatch to Sloan.

"You seem to have forgotten your firearm etiquette, Mr. McKay. That's certainly no way to offer a man a shotgun. Especially one as nasty as that."

McKay held his nose as he tried to stretch his arm through the hatch. "My only regret is that the damn thing isn't longer," he honked.

"I trust it's unloaded," Sloan said.

"Of course it's loaded. And if you get any closer than the length of the barrel I'm gonna pull the goddamn trigger."

Sloan pushed, McKay pulled, and together they managed to heave the naval commander to his feet.

"Are you hurt?"

"Only my pride."

"What the hell were you doing in there in the first place?" McKay asked.

"I was just passing by when Cygnus blew up and knocked me into the head," Sloan explained. "The hatch slammed shut, and I guess the tanks ruptured. I figured since I was already baptized I might as well stay. It was the safest place on the ship, anyway."

McKay decided to buy the explanation mainly because he didn't care whether it made any sense. Besides, he had other things to worry about.

"Where the fuck are we?" he blurted.

"You know, that reminds me of a joke," Sloan said. "There was this tribe in Africa called the—"

"Just tell me where we are, Sam."

"Why, Alaska, ole buddy."

"Yes. I know," McKay groaned. "But *where* in Alaska?"

"The Seward Peninsula, best I can figure it."

"Where's that?"

"Western tip of Alaska," Sloan explained. "Directly across the Bering Strait from Siberia."

"Aren't there supposed to be some commie renegades around here?"

"That's what the reports say."

"Perfect!"

"What are you two doing in there?" Rogers's stuck his head through the main hatch. "Can't you smell the fuel?"

"No!" McKay and Sloan answered in unison.

"Well, take my word for it, it's real. Now grab whatever you can and let's get out of here." Rogers cradled a couple of Franchis and disappeared through the opening.

McKay leaned out of the main hatch. Before him stretched a white plain edged by trees several hundred meters to the east. He smelled the sea and thought for a moment he even heard breakers crashing. Tony and Casey were safely stowed fifty meters away, where they were erecting a "tinfoil" umbrella in the snow, and Rogers was shuttling matériel to them from the ship.

"You take the weapons and ammo, Sam. It doesn't matter what *they* smell like. I'll get the blankets and food." McKay reminded himself that spring in Alaska was like winter almost every place else, and naturally they weren't prepared for it. The Guardians were equipped for orbital combat but not arctic survival. He grabbed several thermal blankets and all the "space food" he could carry.

"What about communications?" Sam asked.

"Casey's taking care of that." McKay hopped the short distance down to the snow-covered ground. "This a small step for man, but a giant step for—"

"Whoomp!" An explosion shook the ground and launched a white plume of snow high into the air.

"What the hell?" McKay twirled around in the snow as if he had one foot nailed to the floor, looking for some sign that would locate the source of the explosion. Then:

"Phump!"

"Mortar!" Sloan yelled from StarVan's hatchway, pointing to the east. "From the tree line!" Then he dove out of the doorway, hit the snow in a tuck and roll, and came up running.

McKay spun in the direction of the trees but didn't have

time to identify anything before he had to hit the ground. The second mortar shell landed dead center on the StarVan, which went up in a fist of yellow, red, and black. Everyone tried to bury themselves in the snow to avoid the white-hot shrapnel.

"Well, there goes the neighborhood, goddammit!" McKay shouted to no one in particular. He started crawling in the direction of Tony and Casey, who were folding up the portable mylar satellite dish. No sense in providing a nice shiny target to zero the mortar in on. McKay arrived at the same time as Sloan and Rogers, which he thought was especially nice since they had the weapons.

"OK, let's inventory," McKay barked, taking command. "What have we got?"

"Four Franchis and fifty rounds apiece," Sloan answered.

"Is that all?"

"One MP5 and ten magazines," Casey added.

"Well, can I assume we've all got our side arms at least?"

"Are you kidding?" Tony piped up. "I'd feel naked without my piece."

"Don't get me started," McKay snorted. "So, everybody's got theirs?"

"Negative." Tom Rogers stared at the snow. Everyone looked at him as if he had just stepped off a spaceship, which, indeed, he had. "I left it at Vandenberg." He looked at the others imploringly. "I didn't think I'd need it!"

McKay rolled his eyes toward the sky. "Any more surprises?"

Silence.

McKay took private stock of the situation: Tony had her Dan Wesson .357 magnum with jacketed loads, the same piece with which she had shot Sylvie Braestrop through the Cygnus fuselage to save the mission and everyone's lives; Casey had his Dirty Harry .44 Mag; Sloan had his nickel-plated Colt Python .357; and McKay patted his hip holster for a tactile reminder that he still had his model 1911 Colt .45 automatic.

"Rounds?"

Tony: "Forty-six."

Casey: "Fifty."

Sam: "Fifty."

McKay had fifty rounds. That was 196 sidearm rounds, 200 shotgun rounds, and 300 rounds for the MP5 machine pistol, which a hot firefight would eat up in about five minutes. That gave them 646 rounds, none of which was effective past 200 meters, to fight god-knows-what-with-a-mortar. *So this is what fucked feels like*, McKay thought.

"Lookie here what I found." Rogers's voice was muffled because he had his head buried in a brigade bag. Then he emerged, like a diver surfacing, and produced a grenade in each hand.

"Stun and white phosphorous," he beamed. "Take your pick."

"How many?" McKay asked.

"Five each."

"Well, I guess that's better than a spot on the lung," McKay mumbled.

"And . . ." Rogers reached back into the bag. "Just the ticket for sophisticated warfare." With a flourish he withdrew his hand, which brandished a short-bladed sword.

"Oh, yes. How could we forget?" Casey spat. "The latest in space-age technology."

McKay smiled. The half-meter blades were especially designed for close combat in a weightless environment and, despite Casey's sarcasm, had proved their effectiveness that very day—though it seemed like a year ago—when the Guardians attacked the Cygnus platform. Like futuristic buccaneers they had launched an orbital boarding party that overwhelmed the Cygnus defenders and cost Yevgeny

Maximov one very expensive and, for the time being, irreplaceable laser cannon. And McKay sneered as he remembered what the attack had cost Dr. John Mallory. Yes, the "space swords" had definitely earned McKay's respect that day.

"Well, maybe they'll come in handy," McKay conjectured. But not, he recognized, as handy as his M-60 machine gun or Casey's Remington sniper rifle or Sloan's Galil SAR with the M-203 grenade launcher mounted under the barrel. This was the Guardian's standard armament, which they had had to leave behind during their space mission. It was something McKay hated to do, but the weight restrictions had forced the decision. "I'll never do that again," McKay swore out loud.

"Me neither." Sloan had read his mind. "The 203 alone would give us a range of 400 meters, almost to the trees. In effect we'd have our own mortar."

"Phump!" That sound again.

"Incoming!" McKay shouted just before he tried to crawl under the snow.

"Whoomp!" The round landed halfway between the smoking remains of the StarVan and the cluster of survivors.

"I got a bad feeling about the next one," Casey muttered.

But there was no next one. Instead the Guardians watched transfixed as a steady line of horsemen emerged like ghosts from the background of the forest.

"What the fuck?" McKay babbled.

"I ain't believin' this," drawled Sloan.

The line of cavalry moved inexorably away from the tree line and toward the Guardians.

"So, what do we do now, Billy?" Casey asked. "Circle the goddamn wagons?"

McKay never heard Casey's remark. He was too busy concentrating on the slivers of steel that flashed in the sunlight just above the horses. This couldn't be happening, he thought, but of course it was.

"Gentlemen," McKay said, "I'm afraid we've just entered the Twilight Zone. Brace yourselves for a full-fledged saber charge."

The Guardians just looked at one another, incredulous.

"Perfect!" they said in unison.

CHAPTER
THREE ——————————————————————

"Ummmh . . . ahhh . . . oh, *mon dieu*."

The moaning would have been more arousing if Yevgeny Maximov hadn't also found it so amusing. *So this is how she makes love*, he thought as he reached to adjust the contrast on the video monitor. The image of a naked Natalie Frechette squirming beneath her lover focused perfectly on the screen.

Every room in the vast Schloss Ehrenbreitstein castle was wired for both audio and video, a fact that was not lost on the French woman currently copulating on closed-circuit television. Though Natalie had disconnected the unit monitoring her bedroom, Maximov had ordered the installation of another secret device within hours of her discovery. It was one of the privileges that accompanied the chairmanship of the Federated States of Europe.

Despite his position, Maximov had never used his power to explore Natalie's anatomy firsthand, though he could have and often fantasized about it. She was, after all, a beautiful woman in her late thirties and at the height of her sexual prowess. And her full, tight body was eminently desirable. But she was too valuable in other areas to risk losing because of some insipid lover's quarrel. Besides, physical pleasure was something Maximov could indulge in elsewhere—anywhere.

"Ooooh . . . ," she gasped as she arched her back and curled her thighs around the rippling torso of the young major who grunted over her like some great blond beast. Maximov allowed himself to twitch slightly when Natalie threw her head back, tossing her hair, which flowed like a river of burnt umber over the pillow, and closing her eyes in ecstasy. Then she bit into her lower lip, drawing a single droplet of blood, which she then licked away.

Maybe I should forego my own rule, the chairman thought, raising an eyebrow. He had always denied himself the pleasures of dipping his wick into staff members, especially those as important as Natalie. As director of the executive committee, she virtually ran the day-to-day operations of the empire and so was almost indispensable to him—almost!

"A touch of the acrobatic." Maximov chuckled as the young officer shifted his weight to his knees and drew Natalie's long legs upright to straddle his muscular chest. Then the chairman laughed out loud when the eager puppy began to gnaw her ankles as he banged frantically away at her, all the while pawing her perfect breasts. With some effort Natalie managed to slow her lover down to a more manageable pace and, after gaining control, began to lightly rake his loins with her razor sharp nails.

"He won't be able to stand much more of that," Maximov snickered. He noticed that the angelic-faced officer was already trembling, and he wondered how much he, too, would be able to endure, even had he been the officer's age. *Not much,* he conceded, trembling himself.

The scene playing out before him provided Maximov with an opportunity to kill several birds with one stone.

First, it allowed him some insight into the *real* Natalie Frechette, without her mask of efficiency that included a severe hairstyle and dowdy clothing, all contrived to give her an absurdly plain appearance. He had always suspected there was a passionate tigress hidden beneath that exterior of cold steel. Now he knew.

It also allowed Maximov to judge his newest creation, who just happened to be the male star of the current broadcast. He had just made Fyodor Petrovsky the youngest major in the short history of the empire. But at twenty-four, he had all the qualifications to lead Maximov's new commando unit—his Serpent Squad especially created to thwart the American Guardians. After three years of failure using conventional methods, Maximov finally decided it was time to fight fire with fire. If a small unit of carefully picked experts could wreak such havoc on his empire, then he, too, should have such a team to return the favor, he reasoned.

And Petrovsky was a perfect choice to lead it. Though he was young, he was also cunning and possessed a streak of cruelty that Maximov admired. Besides, Petrovsky's choir-boy good looks belied his appetite for blood, and his glaring lack of moral responsibility bordered on the sociopathic. This added a twinge of irony that appealed to Maximov. Also Petrovsky had excelled in all the exotic training courses necessary for this sort of work and had distinguished himself during the occupation of America, especially in the realm of special interrogation techniques. *That should come in handy,* Maximov thought and smiled.

And at six-four, 225, Petrovsky certainly appeared to have the physical qualifications for the assignment. *But then,* Maximov mused, *perhaps it would be better to ask Natalie about that.*

The chairman slowly stroked his grizzled beard as he watched the gyrations on the screen. He had always harbored a weakness for voyeurism but never tried to hide it. He considered it a harmless vice, one in which he could indulge without causing any overt harm, which was certainly more than he could say for his other sexual deviations. He thought of little Emily Mallory for a moment and wondered if she would like to watch television this evening. He reached for the remote control wand on the antique table beside him and punched the record button.

He judged that the couple had launched into their final frantic pace leading to orgasm, and he considered whether he should buzz the room just before they peaked. He smiled to himself as he ruminated over the decision. This was all great fun, after all, but there was pressing business to attend.

Just minutes before, Maximov had received a transmission from his tracking station in northwest Spain, one of the few still free of the Islamic hordes who had captured the Mediterranean coast. The message informed him that the La Coruña facility had "lost" the signal from Cygnus X-1.

How does one mislay a signal? Maximov wondered. *Incompetent fools!* He was already planning how he would deal with them. Their only explanation had been that the radar blip had just disappeared, as if it suddenly had been erased. Yet a space platform just doesn't suddenly *disappear*. Unless, of course, President MacGregor had unleashed the Guardians on the space vessel. That was always a possibility, though he thought that particular eventuality had been eliminated. Upon his orders, the Cygnus had used its laser cannon to vaporize Vandenberg, the only U.S. Air Force Base known to harbor an orbiter. The rest had been destroyed in the One Day War. Something had evidently gone wrong, though, and whatever it was reeked of the Guardians. He needed Natalie to check with her assets in Washington to see if his intuition was correct. He would give the lovers a few more minutes of pleasure, but if they could not finish by then, he would have to engage in a little electronic coitus interruptus.

As though she had read her commander's mind, Natalie hooked her ankles around Petrovsky's neck and drew him down to her. He cradled her buttocks in his enormous arms and plunged into her as if trying to rip her apart. Maximov smiled as Natalie groaned in agony, then raised her hips to meet the next thrust. The lovers thrashed and bucked on the satin sheets like two minks in season, their rhythm reaching a fever pitch. Natalie's breath was coming hard and fast now, and Maximov could see that she was racing out of control. Suddenly Petrovsky drew her breast into his mouth and bit down hard on her budding nipple. Natalie threw her head back and screamed, then went rigid in Petrovsky's arms. Every muscle in her body corded as if her climax had paralyzed her. She clung to Petrovsky in desperation, her knees gripping his shoulders, clutching him tightly as spasms rippled through her body. Then she launched a rapid-fire assault with her hips, pumping as hard as she could to prolong the last vestiges of her delirium.

"It's about time," Maximov said as he picked up the phone.

CHAPTER
FOUR

Even through seven-power binoculars Billy McKay still couldn't believe his eyes. He fiddled with the focus just to make sure the instrument was not lying to him. But no matter how he fingered the knob, when the image returned to clarity it was always the same: an unbroken line of guerrillas—bearded, great-coated, and sabered—mounted on horses that pawed at the tundra as they snorted jets of steam like dragons. They pranced in formation at the edge of the forest, waiting for their riders to spur them across the snow-covered plain.

McKay squinted through the eyepieces and saw a red star centered on the upturned flap of the commander's fur hat. He was a burly man with flowing black mustaches that flared like wings from his nostrils. McKay imagined that his great-grandfather probably commanded the czar's imperial guard of mounted cossacks. The man twisted from side to side in his saddle, shouting instructions to his line. *He's the one we need to kill first,* McKay thought, wishing Casey had his Remington M40A1 sniper's rifle. *Casey could*

*probably plant one on the bridge of his nose from here and
end the battle in one shot.*

He panned down the line and counted thirty-one horsemen, all with weapons that had been obsolete for decades.
There were ancient Kalashnikovs, the AKM versions from
the looks of the receivers, some bolt-action jobs that even
he didn't recognize, and a . . . *what the hell?* . . . an
old PPD Model 1940 submachine gun, McKay guessed
from the drum magazine. If he remembered his old weapons
manuals, the PPD had a cyclic rate of 1100 rounds per
minute.

"We'd better take that one out next," he whispered to
himself.

McKay aimed the glasses back at the center of the line
and saw the commander turn toward him and smile as if the
two were separated by just a few feet instead of over four
hundred meters. Then, with a flourish, he drew his saber,
pointed the blade directly at the marine, and let out a silent
shout as the line bolted out of focus. McKay dropped the
glasses to his chest and took in the whole formation as it
thundered toward him.

"Well, guys, I guess it's time to . . ."

He turned to see that he was talking to himself.

"Hey, Zhivago!" Casey yelled. "You'd better get your
ass back here." He was huddled with the rest of the group
behind the tail section of the broken StarVan.

Like a cartoon character, McKay zapped out of frame and
covered the forty meters in a blur. "Thanks for the moral
support, shitheads," he puffed as he dove behind the jagged
piece of fuselage.

Casey's take was a slow burn. "Did you think we were
just going to stand out there and get trampled to death?"

"I was reconnoitering. OK?" McKay explained.

"Can your reconnoitering answer me one question?"
Tom Rogers asked. "Who are these guys?"

"I don't know. Some fucked-up Red Brigade. You tell him, Sam. I ain't got time for no history lesson," McKay snapped as he switched into his command mode. Then he started doling out grenades along with instructions. First, he had everyone inspect their shotgun shells for any slugs that might have slipped in by mistake. The standard issue for the Franchi was number one buckshot, but every once in a while a Brenneke slug would show up. The rifled Brenneke was a bit heavier than its American counterpart and so had a better ballistic coefficient.

"I found a slug," Tony sang out.

"Great!" McKay was cooking now. "Give it to Casey. Tom, you take the MP5. Casey, take the shotgun and the slug."

"I think I'm beginning to get the picture," Casey said.

"It's about fucking time," growled McKay. "Listen up, everybody. Casey's going to drop ol' Taras Bulba there up front, then we let go with the phosphorous grenades—should scare the hell out of any horses they don't kill or blind. Then Tom cleans house with the MP5 while we back him up with the Franchis. Shoot the horses if you have to. Got it?" The last part wasn't really a question.

McKay took Casey aside, gave him the glasses, and pointed out the cavalry leader. "That's your man!"

Casey refocused the Zeiss binocs, then flinched. "He's not really my type, Billy." Magnified seven times, the commander appeared to be snarling about a foot away. Casey lowered the glasses and saw that the charge had covered about half the field. He jacked the slug into the receiver.

"Can you do it?" McKay looked right into his eyes.

"With this piece of shit?" Then he wilted under McKay's stare. "Dunno . . . maybe."

"Maybe?"

"How much room have we got?"

"I saw some AKs," McKay explained. "They're old, but they've got the reach on us, even on horseback. I figure seventy meters, no less."

Casey threw the Franchi to his shoulder and sighted down its ridiculously short barrel. "That would normally be about a two-inch drop. But with this thing, at a moving target?"

"Of course it's not important, Case. It's only life or death."

"I'll see what I can do."

"Good boy." He slapped Casey on the shoulder, then wheeled away.

McKay crabbed down the makeshift line the Guardians had formed behind the crumpled tail section. There wasn't enough of the fuselage left to form a substantial barricade, so the outcome depended on the confusion and damage they could inflict with the grenades. He tucked Tony into the angle formed by the tail fin and what was left of the body, and put Sam on the left flank. Tom and his MP5 were protected in the middle. Then McKay moved to anchor the flank just to the right of Casey. He looked back down the twenty-foot line and saw that everybody was locked and loaded and had grenades handy. They were ready.

McKay surveyed the field. It was the first moment he'd had to really appreciate the dynamics of a cavalry charge, though there were few dynamics left. What had begun as a neat, flanking line of mounted soldiers had degenerated into what looked like a clump of crazed cassocks wildly brandishing their sabers. Shots were already snapping over McKay's head while he stood to the right of the tail, calmly taking in the madness. The communists shrieked their version of the rebel yell as they rumbled to within one hundred meters of the fuselage.

McKay looked over at Casey, who seemed to meld with the barrel of the shotgun he had layed across the tail wing. That was a good sign, McKay recognized. It meant that he had his concentration flowing. He knew that if Casey could drop that maniac up front, it would demoralize those with less than a fanatical courage. And the Guardians were so hopelessly outnumbered that they would be grateful to any of the enemy who chose to run.

The deranged horde stormed to within seventy-five meters, and more shots cracked in the air. Casey took a breath and held it. He had to do it, McKay thought. And he had to do it now!

The stubby scattergun boomed like a cannon, and the blast blew a cloud of dust off the wing of the tail section. Casey jerked backward from the mule-kick of the recoil but maintained a locked brace on the weapon.

McKay looked out across the field in time to see a slab of gore leap from the top of the commander's head just before he somersaulted off the back of his mount. Several comrades nearby instantly reined in their horses and milled around the body of the leader. One actually dismounted, retrieved his commander's headgear, which still contained the top half of his skull, and placed it carefully back on the lolling head.

"Now!" McKay shouted, and all but Casey, who was still tripped out on his shot, hurled grenades at the wall of horsemen. The incandescent copper balls exploded in a starfish of white phosphorous, drenching the attackers in a shower of scorching flakes that clung to their coats, then burned through to their skin. For those who had remained undaunted by the sudden departure of their leader, *this* definitely got their attention.

McKay heard the horses squealing in agony while they bucked and wheeled, throwing their masters to the ground. The hardened guerrillas shrieked like children and stumbled around aimlessly, tearing at their clothing in an attempt to get at their scorched flesh. Some of the men were actually set alight, and they danced about, screaming, waving arms of flame like human torches. It was an enemy in its most desirable state, McKay thought. *Defenseless!*

"Let 'em have it!" he yelled.

Rogers cranked up his limited edition MP5 and sprayed the wild throng with a shower of .45-caliber slugs. Even using controlled bursts, he raced through several 30-round magazines. The weapon's cyclic rate of 600 RPM consumed the rounds faster than a piranha in a feeding frenzy, and pumped lead into the confused mob with a devastating effect. The commies howled in fear and pain as they crouched under the maelstrom like men caught in a swarm of bees. They swatted, ducked, crawled, and rolled in an attempt to escape the furious fire. McKay caught one trying to burrow under his dead horse and severed his spine with a shotgun blast.

Tony shot one just below the right shoulder with her Franchi, tearing his arm off. A river of red flowed from his stump and saturated the ground. The dazed soldier just stood there for a moment, staring first at his gaping wound, then at the stream of blood pouring over his arm, which now lay at his feet. Then he looked at Tony with glazed eyes and dropped like a felled tree.

On the left flank, Sam took his time and nailed each target with one shot. He hammered first those who broke through the white phosporous cloud, taking care not to shoot the horses, which wasn't all that easy with a scatter-gun. Next he picked out those who were on fire and put them out of their misery. Then he turned his attention to Tom's sector but found no targets there.

Rogers knew that with the MP5 his field of fire was the entire battle zone, which he proceeded to hose down with a torrent of lead. And realizing that Casey was still savoring his miracle shot, he started his spray to the right, where McKay would be alone on the flank. He worked his way to Sam's point on the left, lingering a bit in the middle just to give himself a little added insurance, then started back again. By the time he returned to the center it was obvious that the MP5 and the grenades had done their work with a chilling efficiency and that Sam and Tony were just mopping up. The battle had quickly turned into a massacre. Still, the Russians kept coming.

Though he used short bursts, Tom had consumed nine of the ten 30-round clips on his lateral journey, so he decided to switch the MP5's selector to the single-shot position. But when he let off the trigger, the machine pistol continued to spit out rounds on full automatic.

"What the hell?" he yelped, holding onto the weapon as it climbed on its own. Then he realized that the closed bolt configuration plus the 600 RPM cyclic rate had caused the MP5 to heat up so drastically that it was cooking off rounds all by itself. All he could do was hold on as the weapon spewed out the last of its ammunition into the sky.

"Hey, fumblefuck!" McKay roared. "How about a little help here?" He tossed the remark at Casey, who wore the blank look of a man in a trance. "But, please, don't let me interfere with your meditation." Then the marine swiveled and shotgunned a renegade who suddenly leapt up from behind a dead horse. McKay's blast gave a new meaning to the term "chest cavity."

Shooting for Casey bordered on a mystical experience. He used a mixture of zen and yoga to achieve near-perfect relaxation for each shot, but the consequence was that coming down was not an immediate process.

"Perfection," Casey mumbled. Against the background of the firefight it was like a whisper in a storm. Then suddenly he was himself again. "It looks like you're doing all right to me, dude."

McKay dipped behind the fuselage to reload. "A little cover wouldn't hurt."

"You got it!" Casey jumped up, shooting at shadows

through the phosphorous cloud, which hung tighter on the right flank. *Thank God we got the wind on our side*, he thought. Then a hail of bullets sparked off the tail fin and marched down the length of the fuselage, driving the Guardians to the snow.

"Shit!" blurted McKay. He had been searching for that PPD 1940 throughout the firefight but never found it. He assumed, or at least hoped, that it had gone down to the grenades or Rogers's withering fire. But now he knew different. "Where is the damn thing?" he yelled.

Sam indicated he couldn't hear. Unlike the MP5, which had a built-in silencer, the old PPD roared like a chain saw. McKay reached into his breast pocket, switched on his communicator, and signaled the others to do the same. Then he repeated the question.

"Where is it?" McKay spoke normally through the throat mike taped to his larynx, and the Guardians heard his voice as if it were echoing inside their heads through the bone-conduction receivers taped behind their ears.

"*What* is it?" Sam asked from the left flank.

"You wouldn't believe me if I told you. Just find it! McKay knew that would be an easier task to order than to execute, especially in the poor visibility.

The incessant chatter from the machine gun stopped as suddenly as it had begun, and the Guardians, one by one, raised their heads like turkeys, scouring the field for anything that remotely resembled an automatic weapon, or for that matter, anything that moved. A dark blur broke the cloud on the right center, and Sam pounded it twice with his Franchi. Then he saw it was a fallen horse that had tried to get up.

"Shit," he groaned.

The Russian gun started up again, strafing the top of the fuselage and sending the Guardians back to the ground. The 7.66-millimeter rounds stitched a line down the length of the crumpled body, blowing off chunks of metal like shrapnel.

"We need to find this damn thing," McKay shouted. He had already forgotten that they had switched to subvocal communication. His teammates winced and grabbed their ears. Between McKay's shouts and the nerve-splitting cacophony kicked up by the PPD's 1100 RPM, they were grateful for the semipermanent earplugs they wore as standard issue. Still, they wished McKay would shut up.

Then Tony sang out: "Muzzle flash, dead center, twenty meters." She had burrowed through a gap under the belly of the fuselage to spot the fire.

"Trash the fucker, Tom," McKay ordered.

"With what?" Rogers snapped. "I'm empty."

"Perfect," McKay moaned.

"We've got some stuns left." Tom was anxious to redeem himself.

"Then you throw 'em," McKay said. "I ain't movin'."

Just then a new sound was added to the din. It was an oddly muffled crack that came from ground level. Then the PPD stopped.

Silence.

After thirty seconds McKay whispered into his throat mike: "Somebody want to enlighten me?"

"What do you want to know, apehead?" It was Tony.

McKay groaned. "Ah, shit."

"That's right. I pulled your ass out of the fire *again*."

"I guess I won't hear the end of this real soon, will I?"

"Not for the rest of your worthless life."

Why doesn't somebody stick a dick in her mouth? McKay wondered. Then he realized it was because she would probably bite the damn thing off.

After a few more minutes of silence the Guardians rose and ventured cautiously from behind their cover. The phosphorous cloud had completely dissipated, but there was still the haze of battle that hung over the field like a fine gauze. McKay inhaled the acrid sting of cordite mixed with gore that commonly signaled a fresh killing ground. There were also the indescribable odors of pain, fear, and death. Men groaned, animals snorted, and everywhere there was blood, a lake of blood. He stood still for a moment and let his senses drink of a scene that hadn't changed significantly in a thousand years. There was a kind of twisted clarity about a battle field that was both pure and profane. But more than anything, it was McKay.

"Let's put up the antenna and get the hell out of here," he said quietly. Tony and Sam set to the task. Tom and Casey patrolled the field, checking for wounded and shooting those who were hopeless.

"Don't forget the horses," Sam said.

McKay stripped the bodies of weapons, just in case any of the corpses suddenly decided to come back to life, a miracle he had seen before on the battlefields of the Middle East. No point in taking any chances. He found the PPD, and the man next to it had a neat hole in the center of his forehead, the unmistakable signature of Tony's jacketed .357 loads.

"Signal transmitted and received," Sam said. He spoke from twenty meters away, where he and Tony had erected the inside-out mylar umbrella the Guardians used as their portable satellite link.

McKay grunted and reached for a cigar, his first since he had returned to earth. "And?"

"They're sending a copter for us from Nome. It'll be here in just a few minutes."

McKay pulled out his Zippo lighter of antique brass and fired up the Indonesian tobacco. He drew deeply, holding the smoke in his lungs, and enjoyed the rich flavor. He raised the binoculars to his eyes and focused on the mortar implacement at the end of the meadow. The weapon sat there, angled against its buttplate, unattended. He scanned the tree line. Nothing. He exhaled a long sigh of smoke. For the first time in days he felt he could truly relax.

CHAPTER
FIVE ─────────────────────────────

Yevgeny Maximov reclined in his high-backed leather chair and looked out the enormous window constructed into the western wall of the castle. The sky was streaked with a palette of muted colors, the transitions from one to another so deliciously subtle that the scene excited the chairman almost as much as the video performance he had just witnessed in his private quarters. He tried never to miss the glorious spring sunsets for which the Rhine Valley was famous and specifically for which he had had the picture window built.

He looked across the river at Koblenz, a town situated between the mouth of the Mosel and a broad reach of the Rhine. The dying light bathed the ancient buildings in a soft glow that accentuated their medieval origins, and for a moment Maximov was transported in time as he imagined what life would have been like as a feudal lord. Then it occurred to him that it would have been exactly like the life he was living now.

"You called, Your Excellency?" The breathless voice of Natalie Frechette brought Maximov back to the present. He turned to his chief executive and struggled to keep from laughing in her face. She had managed to put on an immaculately pressed uniform but obviously had found insufficient time for the rest of her appearance. Her magnificent auburn hair, usually done up in a severe bun, was hastily pulled back in a ponytail with several strands hanging loose. Her lip was still bleeding, and Maximov thought he noticed red blotches on her neck and face. *You should tell your young major to shave more closely in the future,* he wanted to say.

"My dear, how good of you to come on such short notice." He extended his hand as he moved toward her. "I trust I didn't interrupt anything important?"

"Nothing is more important than your wish, Excellency." Natalie noticed he was staring at her lip, which she touched self-consciously. She felt the sticky-wet blood on her finger, which she immediately hid behind her back, leaving Maximov's arm outstretched in midair. She wiped her finger on the back of her tunic and quickly reached to clasp the hand of her leader, who chose that moment to turn away.

"I've received an interesting cable from La Coruña." He moved behind the enormous mahogany desk that dominated the room. "It says '. . . have lost signal from Cygnus X-1.' What do you make of this?"

"I don't know, Your Excellency. It must be a mistake."

"I certainly hope so, my dear, but I doubt it." He lowered himself into the giant chair without offering Natalie a seat. "I have this unpleasant suspicion that whatever happened is the handiwork of the Guardians."

"But, Excellency, that's impossible." Her voice climbed slightly, and she fought to control it. "You saw the reports yourself. Cygnus destroyed the only orbiter the Americans had remaining."

"The only *known* orbiter the Americans had remaining," Maximov corrected her. "For all we know the Guardians may have built one from scratch. They've accomplished the impossible before."

"I'll have the facts within the hour." Natalie nodded her head in respect and turned to leave, but Maximov stopped her.

"That won't be necessary. I have others working on that. Please sit down." He motioned to the wing-backed chair that faced the desk and, as a further accommodation, changed languages to Natalie's native tongue. "We must proceed on the supposition that Cygnus and all that it means to us has been destroyed. Naturally you will inquire with your assets in place in Washington to confirm this. On the other hand, we must also allow for any contingencies. This includes the unlikely yet possible survival of Dr. Mallory and/or the laser cannon. With either one the Americans can resume their program which the One Day War interrupted two years ago. I'm sure you can appreciate that this eventuality is one that I consider totally unacceptable."

"Yes, Excellency." Natalie self-consciously smoothed away a strand of hair that had fallen over her face.

"Of one thing we can be assured. If there is the slightest possibility that either the laser or Mallory has survived, then President MacGregor will almost certainly dispatch the Guardians on a retrieval mission. If this happens I want to know about it *immediately*. Do you understand?"

"Yes, Excellency."

"Now, to the second item on the agenda. What do you think of Major Fyodor Petrovsky?"

Natalie flushed a dark crimson and went rigid in her chair. "I . . . uh . . . in what sense? I'm not sure what you mean."

Maximov allowed a trace of amusement to flicker across his eyes. "I mean what do you think of Major Petrovsky . . . as a commander, of course?"

"Well, Excellency, he seems exceedingly capable for one

so young." She twisted on the chair as she crossed her long legs, and Maximov wondered if she was actually becoming moist. "He certainly has all the right tools."

"Does he now?"

"Oh yes, Excellency. I think he provides our . . . your . . . organization with some valuable assets."

As much as your ass sits on him, you should know, he thought, barely able to control himself.

"Do you think he is ready for a crucial assignment?" Maximov thought he noticed a certain ambivalence pull at the corners of Natalie's mouth as she mulled over her answer. He took this as a signal that perhaps she harbored real feelings for the boy.

"It is my opinion that he is ready. However I don't know the nature of the assignment," she answered finally.

It is not necessary for you to know, he thought but did not say. "Thank you. I value your opinion."

A low buzz from the intercom signaled the arrival of an important message. Maximov ordered its immediate delivery, and the door opened at once. An officious-looking secretary strode in, placed the folder on the leather blotter, and left, closing the door behind her.

"What have we here?" Maximov said, fumbling for glasses in his breast pocket. He opened the file and read.

"Hm . . . interesting . . . very interesting indeed." He looked at Natalie over the rims of his half-frame spectacles, then closed the file. "It appears that our people at the La Coruña station have lost the signal from Cygnus, all right, but picked up three others in its stead." He removed his glasses and leaned back in the chair. "One of the signals approached from Earth before Cygnus vanished. What does that suggest to you, my dear?"

Natalie leaned forward, propped her elbow on her thigh, and rested her chin on her hand. "This new signal, did it return to Earth after Cygnus disappeared?"

"It appears so, though our tracking device lost contact with it before it landed. The curvature of the earth, you understand."

She nodded that she did. "Then we must assume that the Guardians, or someone, achieved access to another orbiter and destroyed Cygnus. Once again your instincts have proven correct, Excellency."

Maximov allowed himself a slight smile.

"And the other two signals?" she asked.

"They both emanated from the same general position as the platform. One appeared just before and one just after Cygnus's demise, according to this." Maximov tapped the file.

"The one just after was probably a large piece of debris from the explosion. Do you agree?"

"That's a logical assumption," Maximov said.

"That leaves the mystery of the one appearing just before." Natalie's face knotted in concentration. "You indicated it came from the platform itself?"

"Yes."

"Excellency, was there an escape pod aboard?"

"Not to my knowledge." He peered at her over his glasses, with accusing eyes.

"If there was, *I* certainly knew nothing of it." She met his steel gaze with one of her own. Maximov tried to stare her down, but several unsuccessful seconds of this convinced him she was telling the truth. "Mallory?" she asked, finally.

"The inescapable conclusion, if you will pardon the pun."

"Then he *is* alive."

"The probability of this appears to be increasing with every passing second, does it not?"

"Yes, Excellency. I am afraid it does." She slumped in her chair. "Do we know where the pod landed?"

"Not exactly—again the curvature of the earth. But we

do have a computer analysis of the general location based on the re-entry data."

"And that would be?"

"Somewhere in the south-central United States."

"*Mon dieu!*" She gasped as if the knowledge had struck her a blow.

"So you see, my dear, you have work to do. Please contact your assets in Washington at once. We must know the precise location of the pod."

Natalie rose and started for the door. Halfway across the room she stopped and turned toward the desk. "Excellency, if Mallory has fallen into American hands, then what are we going to do?"

Maximov stroked his beard slowly. "Send in Petrovsky, will you?"

CHAPTER
SIX

Dr. John Mallory awakened with a start and screamed into the face of the woman who was gently swathing his brow. She jumped off the edge of the bed and ran out of the room, shouting for someone with initials for a name. Mallory sat straight up and panted fiercely, trying to catch his breath. "Jonesy!" he yelled at the ceiling. All he could think of was the terror of re-entry, and all he could see was Jonesy's head plopped in his lap like some sort of perverse offering.

He raised his head but felt dizzy and quickly lowered it again. His body ached with a pervasive soreness but otherwise he was unhurt. Then the room seemed to move slightly, an almost imperceptible undulation that sent a wave of nausea sweeping over him. Mallory leaned over the side of the bed and vomited. "Shit!"

"Looks like puke to me."

Mallory looked up as a burly, middle-aged man extended a slab of a hand in his general direction. "How's it hangin', man?" he heard him say. Mallory extended his own limp hand and allowed it to be crushed by the shaggy giant who stood over him.

"I'm not certain," Mallory heard himself say.

"Well, I ain't surprised to hear that, considerin' what you've been through," said the bear. "It's just a damn good thing we was close by and could get to you before you drowned." He sat on the edge of the bed, lowering the mattress several inches under his considerable mass. "Damn, we thought the fuckin' Martians was coming or something."

Mallory felt a bit dizzy and so allowed himself to recline. "Unfortunately, I don't qualify as an extraterrestrial."

"You don't talk like no human I ever heard," the bear said. Then he turned toward the door, tilting the mattress at an angle that threatened to send Mallory rolling off the bed. "Rachel, the spaceman had a little accident," he called out. "Could you come clean up the floor, honey? Damn stuff's gettin' all over my boots."

A woman, whom Mallory faintly recognized, entered the room with a roll of paper towels in one hand and a bucket in the other and disappeared below the edge of the bed.

"My name's J. K. Sand, by the way. I suspect yours is Flash Gordon." The man's laugh was as bearish as the rest of him.

"I'm Dr. John Mallory." A slight nod accompanied the name and gave it a touch of formality.

"A doctor, huh? That's great! Can you do abortions?" he blurted. Rachel shot him a malevolent look from the floor.

"I'm a physicist, actually." Mallory was beginning to wonder if perhaps the bear suffered from some congenital brain disorder. "Where am I?"

"Indian Bay."

Mallory thought about that for a moment, then tried to place the man's peculiar accent. "Australia?"

"No, man, Arkansas! You're back in the good ol' U. S. of A."

Christ! Mallory thought. *Of all the places on the globe, I have to land in America.* Then he remembered the merciless shower of death he was forced to unleash on Vandenberg from orbit. As an extra portion of punishment, Maximov had ordered the family quarters of the air force base destroyed, and Mallory complied by carving up the innocents with his laser scalpel as neatly as any sadistic surgeon. *When they find out what I've done,* he thought, *they'll probably cut my balls off.* "How fortunate for me," he said.

"Yeah, it could have been worse. You could have landed in Europe. Then the Effsees would own your ass."

"That would be depressing," Mallory said, thinking that at least in Europe he wouldn't be considered a mass murderer. And he would be closer to his daughter and so would have a better chance of effecting her release.

"What were you doin' up there in that thing, anyway?" J.K. asked.

Mallory considered his answer carefully. "Research," he said finally.

"What kind of research?"

"Uh . . . research pertaining to . . . oh . . . the effects of light on solid matter in a weightless environment."

The bear scratched his head. "And what did you learn, that it shines?" His laugh was like a small roar.

"Yes . . . that's about it," Mallory faked laughing with him.

"You work for NASA then, don't you?"

"Yes, that's right. NASA."

"You NASA boys are weird," J.K. said. "And you sure talk funny. Where're you from?"

"Originally? Ireland. But I've been living in . . . uh . . . Houston lately." He pronounced it House-ton.

"I hear there ain't a whole lot left of *House-ton* since the war. And nothin' left of NASA."

"Yes, well, they've been doing a lot of rebuilding."

"Hmph," J.K. grunted.

"You said something earlier about drowning?" Mallory changed the subject. "Did I touch down on water?"

"You sure did. Smack in the middle of Indian Bay."

"Strange, I don't remember any of that."

"I don't blame you."

"But the pod is airtight and is fitted with a flotation collar. How could I have been in any danger of drowning?"

"Because, Dr. Mallory, you came out of that capsule like a Brahma out of a chute. And you was waving this head around and screaming like a banshee. You went berserk and jumped out of the capsule into the water. We just barely got to you in time."

Mallory winced as the memories flooded back.

"You were yellin' about killing somebody named McCoy, or something."

"McKay." Mallory gritted his teeth.

"Is he the one the head belongs to?" J.K. asked. "Did you kill him?"

"No."

"Who's Jonsey? You called that name out several times, too." Mallory's expression let J.K. know that the name and the head belonged to the same man. "I see."

The room moved again and startled Mallory. "What the Christ is that?"

"That's Indian Bay. You're sittin' on it. Or lyin', rather." Mallory hoped he meant the first definition of the word.

"We're on a ship, then?"

"A converted paddle wheeler—you know, a steamboat. It's a sort of a houseboat now."

"In a place called Arkansas?"

"You never heard of it?"

"Well, yes, of course. But I'm not certain as to its exact location."

"It's just northeast of Texas," J.K. explained. "You know, where *House-ton* is?"

"That's right. Of course," Mallory fumbled. "I'm still a bit confused—the shock and all." He gestured with his hand to indicate that he was not all there.

"What happened?"

Mallory wondered how much he should tell him. "I'm not sure. The heat shield was damaged . . . the control panel exploded . . . the entire incident was very upsetting."

J.K. smiled at the understatement. "Well, I guess you NASA boys can fuck up just like the rest of us."

"Yes."

Rachel rose from the floor. "Next time he pukes, you clean it up." Then she turned and stalked out of the room.

"Don't mind her," J.K. apologized. "She's just coming down."

"Coming down?"

"You know, from a trip."

Mallory wondered if Rachel was suffering from jet lag.

"She dropped some primo acid about thirty-six hours ago," J.K. explained. "It's starting to wear off now, though."

"Acid?"

"You know: album covers, microdots, blotter, Purple Haze, Sunshine—acid, man—LSD!"

"Oh." Mallory remembered a few of the archaic terms from his youth. "D-lysergic acid diethylamide. A hallucinogenic substance."

"You got it, dude. Psychic ambrosia."

Mallory now understood that J.K.'s peculiar mental process was not the result of a congenital defect but rather was chemically induced.

"And that's the end of it," J.K. added. "The bitch polished off the last blotter, and there ain't no more to be had."

"Hey, J.K.?" A man with a shock of coal-black hair and a graying beard popped his head through the door. Mallory could hear, but not see, that there were others with him. "We're all finished. Is he ready?" He nodded toward Mallory.

"We'll be there in just a little bit." J.K. answered, and the man disappeared.

"Are we going someplace?" Mallory asked.

"Oh yes."

"I'm afraid that's impossible. I don't feel up to moving about just yet."

"I figger you've recovered enough for this."

"What?"

"Kind of a going away party."

"If you don't mind, I'd prefer to forgo the festivities.

"But you don't understand, Doctor. You *are* the festivities." J.K.'s expression shifted suddenly from that of an amiable cub to a full-grown, pissed-off grizzly, and Mallory felt a heavy dose of paranoia ripple through his brain.

J.K. stood up and glowered down at the prostrate physicist. "You hi-tech boys are the ones who got us into this mess in the first damn place. You worship sophisticated equipment that never works, and when it breaks down, half the world dies. You think your fancy degrees give you the right to play geopolitical games, or whatever you call them. But when they get out of hand, it's other people who pay the price. Now, it's your turn to pay."

Mallory fought to retain his composure. "With what currency do you propose I perform this payment?" he said as coolly as he could.

"Hey, you're the rocket scientist, Doc. You figure it out."

The dark-haired man stuck his head back through the door. "We got the cross all built and ready to go, man." He did a little shuffle in the doorway. "Let's rock 'n' roll!"

"Cross?" Mallory blanched.

"Just think of it as a religious ceremony." J.K. smirked.

Unthinkable images began to formulate in Mallory's imagination, but they were too grotesque to grasp. When the idea finally crystallized in his brain, he went numb. "You're not actually thinking in terms of a formal crucifix-ion, are you?"

"Oh, no, Doc. It's strictly casual. Come as you are sort of thing."

Mallory shot up in bed and ineffectually tried to claw his way past J.K., but the bear easily slapped him down with one giant paw.

"There's no sense in you trying to go anywhere, Doc. There's nowhere to go, and I've already seen how good you can swim. So you just rest easy, and I'll come back for you in a little while. Try some of this." J.K. reached in his shirt pocket and withdrew a marijuana cigarette the size of a Tiparillo. "It'll make the whole thing go so much easier."

Mallory benignly accepted the gift, which included a pack of matches, and watched, stunned, as the giant lumbered out of the room. He fired up the joint and took an enormous hit, which launched him into a violent coughing attack. When the spasms subsided he looked at the joint, then placed it on the table beside the bed. For a moment he just lay there, still as a stone. Then he pulled the covers up over his head. "Jaysus," he whimpered.

CHAPTER
SEVEN ─────────────────────────

It had to come sooner or later, and when it did it came with a vengeance. World War Three only lasted one day, but it killed more people than both its ancestors and all its piss-ant cousins spread out over the twentieth century—combined! Two hundred forty million deaths were suffered by the two major combatants alone—one hundred ten million Americans against one hundred thirty million Russians. And the carnage in the remainder of the world from direct blasts and fallout, not to mention fire, starvation, disease, and murder by desperation and rage, was simply God's guess.

And yet it was this One Day War, the apocalypse, that had spawned the Guardians like devil dogs from the loins of hell. They were created out of the fear of it and launched into action out of its terrible reality. Their Lucifer was Major Crenna, a one-eyed, half-faced gargoyle who put them through a new version of Hades hidden somewhere deep in the Arizona desert. There they trained like animals until their physical skills were honed to a scary edge. They drilled for every possibility until their expertise covered the

*full spectrum of specializations—from computer program-
ming to satellite communications to Tai Kwon Do to the
proper methods of performing a perfect evisceration. And
when that inevitable, horrific day arrived, they were ready.*

But they weren't ready for the curve ball thrown by their
commander in chief and the cardinal purpose for their
existence. The Guardians had been set up as an elite
four-man unit with the specific responsibility to safeguard
the chain of command of the leadership of the American
government—primarily the President of the United States—
in the event of a thermonuclear exchange. But on the day
the shit hit the fan, President William Lowell boarded his
personal UH-60 Blackhawk transport helicopter and politely but summarily dismissed his protectors with the words
"From here on I'll be in the hands of God and the U.S. Air
Force." Then he whirled away toward Andrews Air Force
Base, where he joined his cabinet aboard the National
Emergency Airborne Command Post (NEACP-2), a converted 747 in which the country's leaders were to ride out
the coming firestorm in presumed safety.

This left the Guardians with a secondary mission to
protect Vice-President Jeffrey MacGregor, an amiable and
able young man, but one who paled by comparison to the
larger-than-life President Lowell. The assignment repre-
sented a comedown for the Guardians, who, after months of
rigorous training, openly resented the change.

Then a quirk of history produced a group of revolution-
aries who fired one rocket that reversed the turn of events.
Québecois separatists shot down NEACP-2, and President
Lowell along with his entire cabinet plummeted from
thirty-five thousand feet up in the Canadian sky. Within
minutes MacGregor was sworn in as president, and the
Guardians were back in the driver's seat—literally.

The first order of business was to bundle up the new
president in Mobile One, the Guardians' specially modified

armored personnel carrier, and get him safely out of the mostly destroyed and completely deranged capitol. They shot their way out of Washington, D.C., forced to kill their own countrymen, who lashed out in fury at anyone even suspected of being a government official. The Guardians' destination was a secret command bunker, called the Heartland, buried deep in the fields of Iowa. There they deposited their package and settled in for the comfort and safety of a long winter's nap. But comfort and safety just weren't in the plan.

For the better part of the next two years the boys wandered across the country on a quest to retrieve the hidden pieces of a very special puzzle. Dubbed the Blueprint for Renewal, this puzzle was a plan for the rebuilding of America. Without these programs, texts, passwords, and critical pieces of hardware buried all over the nation, the giant computers of the Heartland couldn't put the U.S.A.'s shattered skeleton back together again.

The boys completed their mission, which ironically included the destruction of the Heartland with Major Crenna trapped inside. President Lowell, who had miraculously survived the crash in Canada only to trade his good fortune for a life of safety and subjugation to Chairman Maximov, also perished in that nuclear explosion, which lit up the Iowa countryside like a nova.

With the Blueprint for Renewal Safely intact and the country on the mend, the Guardians turned their attention to expelling the invading forces of the Federated States of Europe, Chairman Maximov's gang of uniformed cutthroats. After kicking ass and taking names among the Effsees, the Guardians became President MacGregor's private force of elite troubleshooters. Their duty was to protect the once-superpower-now-fledgling-nation from such threats as orbiting laser beams, which is why they were playing around in space just before their Alaskan adventure. It was a strange gig, they knew. But it was their gig and they were good at it. Besides, it beat the hell out of a regular job.

"You gotta be shittin' me!" McKay cradled the back of his neck with clasped hands and raised his head off the armored plating of Mobile One's front deck. "Mallory's alive?"

"We don't know, at least not for certain." Dr. Lee Warren placed a Reeboked foot on the edge of the giant blade-ribbed tire and grabbed a handful of the nylon webbing that laced the cargo hold of the C-130. The obese bottle-nosed craft dipped through an air pocket, and Warren slipped. McKay suppressed a smile as he watched the suave scientist dangle from the fuselage for an instant. The doctor may be all charm in a lecture hall full of sexy coeds, McKay thought, but in *his* world, the darling of the scientic community was just another clown. Still, he couldn't help but like the man, even if he did dish out a ration of shit.

Warren regained his footing but, in the process, banged his shin against Mobile One's steel hull. "Christ!"

McKay smiled "Damn, Doc. That looks painful to me."

Warren hopped around in the small space formed by the fuselage of the C-130 and Mobile One, wincing. McKay's only regret was that it wasn't Tony Lee hobbling in pain instead of Doc. But they had culled her in Wyoming, where they picked up Warren and the refurbished Mobile One.

The V-450 armored personnel carrier dwarfed the cargo hold of the Super Hercules, leaving scant room for passengers. In an attempt to find comfort, the aircrew and the Guardians draped themselves over and around the cara-paced behemoth like snakes sunning on a triceratops. A loadmaster perched his butt on a corner of the turret and stretched his legs out toward the Herc's frame, hooking his heels over a stirrup cable. To McKay he appeared to hang suspended in an invisible hammock, sound asleep. *How can they do that?* he wondered, as he squirmed about in search of a position less painful than the last.

"What makes you think Mallory might be alive?" Sam Sloan twisted on a pile of duffels near the bulkhead. "Cygnus blew apart, Doc, and I got a shit-stained jumpsuit to prove it."

Tom Rogers grunted a confirmation from the rear deck of the APC.

"Oh, there's no doubt of that, Commander. We saw the platform's signal disappear on the scope. But something else showed up just before Cygnus went out." Warren had finished his little jig and was now softly rubbing his shin. "We think the new signal might have been an escape vehicle of some kind."

"But you don't know who or what escaped," McKay said.

"Right."

"And you tracked this signal, of course?"

"No, McKay. We just let the most dangerous threat to the country since the One Day War return safely to earth without so much as a second look." Warren fixed the marine with a sarcastic sneer. "Of course we tracked it, jarhead!"

"How's the shin, doc?" McKay shot back. Warren touched his leg in an unconscious reply.

"So where are we headed?" Sloan asked.

"Thirty-four degrees, twenty-five minutes north, by ninety-one degrees west."

"Okay, I give up," McKay chimed.

"Somewhere in the lower Mississippi valley?" volunteered Sloan." I'd say Coahoma County."

"Coa-who?" It was McKay again.

"Coahoma County," Warren repeated. "You're close, Sam, but no cigar. It's actually Monroe County."

"Mississippi?"

"No, Arkansas."

"Arkansas?" McKay asked. "Where the fuck is that?"

"Your ineptitude at geography is exceeded only by your lack of couth, Billy."

McKay rolled a quarter turn and farted. "Thanks, Doc."

"So what's the plan, Stan?" Casey Wilson bounded down the steps from the flight deck. He shoved his Who World Tour '89 ball cap to the back of his head and grinned at the group. McKay could tell from the smile that Casey had just come from the left seat up top. The fighter jock couldn't stand merely to ride in an airplane—he had to fly the damn thing. It wasn't that he didn't trust the crew, it was just that he hungered for the tug of the wheel. The Super Herc may not have been an F-18, but it was a bird, and Casey could, and would, find a way to fly any bird ever built.

"We're going after Mallory again," Rogers deadpanned.

"Back in space?" Casey beamed. "Far out!"

"Planet Earth, calling Casey. Come in, Casey—and think about it for a minute." McKay rolled his eyes.

"What?"

"Ah shit, Case. Get real."

"Cut him some slack, Billy," said Sloan. "The boy likes to swoop."

"He's got his head in the clouds, literally," McKay said. "Look, Casey. We're going down, not up, to find Mallory or whoever or whatever and end this shit once and for all. Got it?"

"Jesus, what did I do?"

"You didn't do anything, kid," Rogers said softly. "We just all need a rest, that's all."

Casey shrugged, then threaded his way toward Mobile One, giving McKay a wide berth as he passed. He inspected the cables that fastened the armored beast to its pallet, making sure they were taut. Then he climbed up onto the turret and checked out the ordnance. He ran his hand over the stubby barrel of the M-19 automatic grenade launcher, the vehicle's persuader piece, then checked out the accompanying Browning M-2HB .50-caliber coaxial machine gun. He look contented.

McKay watched the ritual from his new spot against the bulkhead. Casey did this every time they embarked, so it had become sort of an unofficial good luck charm. From the turret he moved to the engine well, popped the hatch, and peered in at the giant V-8 diesel. This was, for all practical purposes, Casey's engine. He was the team driver and mechanic, though Sam helped him with the maintenance sometimes. But whether the engine performed at its peak, which could determine whether they survived, was Casey's responsibility, and he reveled in it.

McKay watched the boy-wonder at work and couldn't help remembering the first time he had ever seen him—two years and three lifetimes ago. He had been just as open and even cockier then, fresh off a hero's reception at the White House. Lt. Kenneth C. Wilson, USAF, enjoyed the full VIP treatment upon his return from combat in the Middle East. A few days before he had smoked *five* Mig 23s over the Gulf of Aden to become the highest-scoring ace since the Korean War. He already had notched two Migs before that incredible day, to bring his total to seven, two more than the record for any airman and a bunch more than any pilot. He had been twenty-eight then but looked younger. His sun-bleached blond hair and surfer's tan probably had something to do with that—at least the girls thought so. They hung on him like he was a rack. Or maybe it was his background. The son of a pair of successful "techies," Casey seemed just naturally raised for the carefree life. But that didn't explain his intensely competitive nature. Casey was the only candidate ever to wash out of aggressor school for being *too* aggressive, a fact that was not lost on McKay. Case got back in on a special recommendation from one of his instructors, a hotshot himself, and toned down his act enough to complete the training and find a home in the cockpit of an F-18. The rest was pure glory.

Maybe I should ease up on him, McKay thought, figuring that Rogers was right. He almost always was. It was odd that Tom Rogers would come to Casey's rescue. The two couldn't be further apart on the human spectrum. Tom was as low key as Casey was brash, but then he was older. At thirty-five he was the senior member of the team, and though not the leader, he acted as unofficial father figure. Everyone, including McKay, just accepted it as the natural order of things.

After all, Rogers had served all over the globe after joining the Army as a kid. He lied about his age, split school, and headed off to see the world at seventeen. The journey took him to every backwater breeding ground for revolution known to exist including Iran, Latin America, Cambodia, and, some say, even the USSR. McKay smiled to himself. Only Rogers would jump into Russia without giving it a second thought.

Nothing scared him. At five-eight, one-eighty, Rogers was built like a fireplug and was just as solid. His sandy blond hair was thinning in front, and that softened his look somewhat, which meant serious trouble for anyone who mistook that for an indication of weakness. Of everyone on the team, Rogers was the only one McKay feared in open combat. Tom had lived for years, cut off from the regular chain of command, surviving off his own resourcefulness. And the life had made him hard.

But his square jaw anchored a face creased with the agony of the Third World. Every peasant ever fucked over by either side lived in his gun-metal eyes. The Special Forces trained him well as an expert cadre, but they couldn't train his heart not to care. Often Rogers would retreat deep inside himself and not speak for days, and McKay wondered if the price had been worth it. But he never had to wonder whether he could count on him.

Rogers's reticence was offset by Sam Sloan's ebullience. A product of the Ozark foothills, Comdr. Samuel Gibbons Sloan made it to the Guardians by way of the U.S. Navy and the Gulf of Sidra. On patrol off the Libyan coast, Sloan's cruiser took a direct hit from a missile that erased the bridge of the USS *Winston-Salem*. All his superior officers were wiped out, so Sloan took command and wrestled the crippled cruiser to port, beating back a series of surface and air strikes. His spectacular work caught the attention of the media, who wasted no time in turning him into a national hero, just as they had done with Casey. Sam knew it was all bullshit, but he wasn't stupid enough to turn down all the adulation. After the free hotels and PR tours subsided, he looked around for another assignment and found nothing that promised anything remotely like the adrenaline rush he had just experienced—until the Guardians' Project came along.

McKay had strong doubts about Sam at the beginning. Why would anyone with half a brain choose a naval commander for a basically land-oriented operation? It just didn't make any sense. But when the training began, and McKay saw how much Sam knew about electronics, communications, and computers, he finally understood. Besides, by then he had grown to respect the Tom Selleck look-alike with the amiable character and soft Southern wit.

"What do you think, Casey? Will they work?" Sloan knelt next to the jet jockey by the front right wheel well of Mobile One. They were inspecting the new amphibious modifications to the vehicle. While the Guardians starcruised for lasers, Washington had dispatched a crew to retrieve Mobile One from a stream in Wyoming, fix its broken fuel pump, and alter the vehicle for water work.

"I don't know," Casey said. "Everything looks tight, but we'll just have to wait and see how she does." Special interior skirts had been welded to the inside of the wheel wells to seal off the front end, and the exhaust system had gotten a new, vertical extension. Two powerful Jacuzzi thrusters had been attached to the rear as a steering aid and optional power source in the water. Since the basic design was an updated version of the old V-150 Commando, which came stock with a barge hull, no other modifications were necessary—theoretically. All of the changes added a mere five-hundred pounds to the machine's ten-ton bulk.

"Well, we'll know in a little while," Sloan said. The pitch of the props changed noticeably as the Super Herc began its descent.

"Saddle up, boys," McKay hitched up his gear and took command. "Ten minutes to show time." He sidled on over to the group. "Tom, I think Dr. Warren has something for you."

Rogers looked up with surprise. "Me?" His expression revealed that he was unaccustomed to receiving anything from anybody. McKay guessed that Tom might have spent his entire sixteen years in the service without once getting a letter.

"General Ebersole of Vandenberg asked me to give you this," Warren said. He thrust out a shoebox with the word Capezzio printed on the top.

"What the hell?" Tom said. He opened the box and broke into a wide grin. I'll be damned." He reached into the box and withdrew an olive-drab holster filled with a Browning high power 9-mm automatic pistol.

"And don't lose it!" McKay barked.

Rogers flushed with a mixture of delight and embarrassment. "I'll guard it with your life," he said.

McKay turned to Warren. "So, what's the drill on Mallory?"

"The usual. Discover what he's up to, find him, and stop him."

"How?"

"Anyway you can."

"Anything else?"

"Find out if the laser survived. If so, get it, too. Or, failing that, destroy it."

"Sounds simple enough."

"Even for a Cro-Magnon, like you?" Warren extended his hand.

"How's the shin, Doc?" McKay smiled.

"Could somebody please tell me why the hell we're doing this?" It wasn't a whine exactly, because Sloan didn't whine. But it was the next thing to it.

"Because we don't want anyone to see us jump," McKay's explanation squelched through the headset.

"Then why don't we *land* like normal troops?"

"We're not normal," Casey stated matter-of-factly.

"We can't just set her down on a field somewhere in broad daylight. Most of the fields are spiked anyway, and all the good ones are being watched. Satisfied?" McKay closed the subject.

"No." Sloan was dangerously close to sulking now. "This is insane."

The Guardians sat patiently inside Mobile One. They were all buttoned up and strapped in and just waiting for the big jolt. There really wasn't anything else they could do. Then static crackled in their ears as someone plugged into the commo system through the exterior port in the hull.

"Good afternoon, ladies and gentlemen. This is your captain speaking." It was Major Miles Gentry from the cockpit of the C-130. "I'd like to take this opportunity to welcome you aboard Grab-Your-Ankles Airlines, and I hope you've enjoyed the flight so far."

"Oh, Christ," Sam moaned.

"As most of you know, our featured entertainment this afternoon will be a LAPES drop of a 20,000-pound APC upon the water. To my knowledge this has never been done before, certainly not by me . . ."

"Shit!" Sam said.

". . . and, as an added attraction, the APC will be loaded with its full complement of crew. Let's hear it for the brave young lads in the back." The sound of yells, whistles, and applause poured over the headset. Mad Miles had his whole crew in on it. "Now for those of you blissfully ignorant of the procedure, allow me to explain. First, LAPES is an acronym that stands for Low Altitude Parachute Extraction System. Under normal circumstances this is considered the single most dangerous procedure performed by the Tactical Airlift Command. But execution of this maneuver over water, and with a human drop, elevates to an even higher figure the already astronomical odds for disaster. And it suggests some serious questions be raised regarding the sanity of the person who ordered this mission."

"You're dead meat, Warren, you hear me?" Sam was getting testy.

"Now for the logistics. We will approach the drop zone at an altitude of two hundred feet and at a speed of one hundred and thirty knots. At approximately four hundred meters from the target we will descend to an altitude of ten feet, a move that is not unlike crashing into a spot."

"Goddammit!" Sloan hissed.

"We will then deploy the canopies, and you will exit the aircraft through the rear ramp just like you were being shot out of a cannon. With any luck, we will then climb safely out of the extraction zone while in all probability you will drown. This is, of course, presuming you are not first killed by the drop itself."

"Will somebody please shut this bastard up?" Small beads of perspiration began to dot Sam's ashen face.

"And now, as a prelude to this afternoon's entertainment, kindly bow your heads and join Master Sergeant Animal Bukowski as he leads us in a stirring rendition of the Lord's Prayer:

'Our fodder, who art . . .'"

McKay sensed his trepidation level rising a few notches but felt better when he looked over at Casey, who was weeping with laughter. Rogers remained impassive, and McKay wondered if he was even wearing his headset. Sloan was clawing at his seat belt.

"'. . . for dine is da kingdom, da power, and da glory, forever and ever. Amen.'

"And remember, folks," Gentry returned, "fly Grab-Your-Ankles Airlines and get fucked every time!"

"Twenty seconds to drop," came another voice over the headset.

"Settle down, Sam," McKay said. "We've done this a hundred times."

"Not like *this* we haven't. Not strapped into the damn thing."

"Fifteen seconds to drop. Deploy drogue."

McKay felt a sharp tug from the rear and noticed the aircraft was dropping rapidly.

"Drogue deployed."

"Green light!"

Then came the pop of the main chute, followed by a rumble that accelerated instantly into thunder, then a yank that relegated rocket thrusters to the laughable. Then came the heaviest rush that Billy McKay had ever felt on or off the planet.

CHAPTER
EIGHT

Mallory threw off the covers and sprang out of bed. He had finally decided he would be damned before he would lie passively by and wait for some village idiot to collect him for crucifixation. The phrase "Are you a man or are you a mouse?" crossed his mind. Then he thought it might be more rational to opt for the mouse if it meant he would escape being nailed to a cross. A cold shudder rippled up his spine as he visualized a procedure that, he suddenly decided, had kindled a renewed respect for Jesus Christ. And now that his religion was intact, Mallory decided he would get the hell out of there before the rest of him came unglued.

He saw there were no windows, or portholes as he seemed to remember they were called on ships, so he tiptoed over to the slatted door and tried to peer between the cracks. He couldn't see much, but he could tell there was some sort of movement on the other side because light and shadow displaced one another at indeterminate intervals. He screwed up his courage and tried the knob. It twisted more loudly than he had hoped. *Damn!*

71

"You wouldn't be trying to go nowhere now would you, Doc?"

Mallory couldn't recognize the voice that was muffled through the wood. As he slunk away from the door he wondered how many of these people there actually were.

He heard a machine that sounded like a chain saw glide past on the opposite side of the boat, then felt that odd undulation that always threatened to bring on nausea. He gripped the bedstead and waited for the feeling to pass. Then another voice, no, more than one, came from beyond the door, and Mallory felt the icy clamp of panic grip his bowels. *My god, they've come for me!* He raced about the room looking for something, anything that appeared to offer even a remote method of escape. With no other option available, he finally slithered under the bed like a snake.

From his vantage point at toe level, Mallory saw the bottom of the door slowly swing open and a pair of smallish bare feet pad into the shaft of light and stop.

"Doctor?" It was an odd, high-pitched whisper. "Doctor, where are you? I've come to get you out of here."

Mallory couldn't believe what he was hearing. Was this an Angel of Mercy sent from the Father as a reward for his recent renewal of faith? The bare feet seemed to suggest so. Still, it was too much for the cynical mind of a trained scientist to grasp. Then he thought perhaps the one drag of marijuana had triggered some sort of latent hallucination that was just now manifesting itself.

"Goddammit, Doctor. We don't have much time."

Fuck it, Mallory thought. *I'm going.* He rolled out from under the bed like a human log. He looked up and saw the upside-down face of an American youth, a boy of about twelve years.

"Dr. Mallory?" the boy said.

"Mr. Stanley, I presume," Mallory replied.

"Huh?" The boy scratched his head. "Come on, let's get

out of here!" He reached down for Mallory's hand and
pulled the doctor up with surprising strength. Then he
jerked him through the door. There was no one outside the
room, so the pair walked quickly toward the hatch at the end
of the hallway.

"What happened to the guard?" Mallory asked.

"Shoooosh!" The boy placed a finger in front of his lips.

"What happened to the guard?" This time Mallory was
careful to whisper.

"I told him J.K. wanted to see him below," the boy said
in a muffled voice. "I lied."

"And may the Holy Virgin bless you for it, my son."

"Huh?"

"Never mind. Where are we going?"

"Just follow me."

"Hey?" Mallory grabbed the boy's arm before he could
spin away. "What's your name?"

"Woody," he said, then he turned, opened the rear door
a crack, peered out, and signaled the 'all clear.'

That's a good strong name, Mallory thought. Then he
followed the boy out into the spring night and to freedom.

Mallory stood on the upper deck overlooking the stream
and sucked in a chestful of the dark rich air. It was his first
outdoor breath of the earth's atmosphere—at least that he
could remember—since he had landed. The water below
slid by like a river of ink in the night, and he wondered why
they called it a bay when it obviously was really just a
stream, and a small one at that.

Woody grabbed his arm, and together they crept down a
set of iron steps that descended to the lower deck of the
vessel. At the bottom the boy heard soft voices and stopped
suddenly. He pointed to two men who sat on the stern near
the paddle wheel passing a joint back and forth. He signaled
to the opposite side of the boat, just beyond the smokers,

indicating that was where they needed to go. Why, Mallory couldn't guess. It looked like open water to him, and open water was not his favorite thing. Woody whispered that he would distract the men while Mallory sneaked over to the other side and waited for him. Mallory nodded that he understood.

The boy popped up whistling and sauntered toward the two men who were trying to pinch a gungi roach into a tiny alligator clip. "Howdie, Tom. Lloyd." Woody nodded.

"Hi there, Woodrow," Tom replied. "What's happening, boy?"

"Ah, not much. Just thought I'd take a peek at the sky and see what stars are out."

"You're a regular little star-freak, ain't you?" Tom finally clipped the butt and took a deep hit, singeing his mustache. "You'd better watch that shit around J.K." His voice sounded surreal as he tried to talk and hold his breath at the same time. "You know how he feels about anything that has to do with science." He passed the clip to the other man, who came dangerously close to inhaling the fiery stub.

"Yeah, I know. But the stars are so fascinating."

"J.K.'ll fascinate your ass if he catches you studying 'em," Lloyd said. "Want a hit?" He offered the clip.

"No thanks. I prefer the stars," he said. Then he pointed into the sky. "Just look up there. Now you see that star? That's Sirius, the brightest star there is. It's 8.6 light-years away and . . ."

The lad truly knows his stars, Mallory thought as he crouched and duck-walked along the trash-filled deck, keeping one eye on the two men and one on his path. He had made it almost to his destination at the far end of the deck when he hooked his foot on an iron cleat and pitched forward in the dark. "Shit!"

"What was that?" Tom turned toward the sound.

"What?" Lloyd said.

Woody jumped in: "I didn't hear anything."

"It came from over there," Tom pointed in the direction of the spot where Mallory lay in the dark, wincing.

"What's that dope your smokin'?" Woody asked.

"I don't know," Lloyd said. "But it's sure good shit. This is the best light show I ever *seen*."

Woody pointed quickly back into the sky. "Now over there, that's Alpha Centauri. You can tell right off it's not as bright as Sirius even though it's twice as close."

Tom turned around and craned upward. "Far out."

Mallory held his breath. The instep of his right foot throbbed mercilessly with every heartbeat, and he was afraid he might cry out in pain. Still, he marveled at how coolly Woody performed under pressure. *I'll have to recruit that lad, he thought. Perhaps even introduce him to Emily.*

". . . and tomorrow night I'll show you the constellations." Woody was winding down. "But I gotta go run some trotlines now." He started off in Mallory's direction. "Good night!"

"Hey, boy," Tom called after him. "You best not be out on that water at night."

"Got to. Momma wants a catfish for dinner, and I promised her."

"But we're goin' to have a crucifixion," Lloyd blurted. "You don't want to miss *that*!"

Mallory gulped.

"I've seen plenty of them," Woody replied.

"I can't let you go, Woodrow." Tom started after the boy. "J.K. would have my ass if I let you on that water after dark."

"It's OK, really! J.K. said I could." He started to backpedal away from Tom.

"Wait a minute." Tom quickened his pace. "What are you up to, boy?"

"Nothin'."

"Lloyd, come over here," Tom said, and Lloyd moved in his direction. "There's something funny goin' on." The two men closed in on Woody and back him up against the rail on the port side.

Mallory crouched in the darkness a yard away from the boy's feet and tried not to breathe. He hoped the groan of the ancient paddle wheel, turning slowly in the current just a few feet away, covered the pounding of his heart. He could tell that Woody's nerve also was starting to crack as he listened to the twelve-year-old fumble with excuses.

Mallory's hand twitched from fear and touched something hard and heavy on the deck. He tried to visualize it with his fingers like a blind person. It was a solid cylinder over a foot long, he guessed, and had several curved hooks on one end and a slender rope tied to the other. He didn't know what the rope was attached to. The object felt as if it were made of lead.

"You're actin' awfully suspicious," Tom said. "What are you hidin'?" He reached out toward the boy.

"Nothin'," Woody insisted, drawing back, but a quiver of panic tinged his voice.

Suddenly the high-pitched clang of a ship's bell shattered the evening stillness. From the bow came a shout: "Prisoner's escaped!"

Oh, shit! Mallory cringed.

"What the hell?" Lloyd looked around.

Tom reached for the .38 holstered in the small of his back. "So that's it, you little bastard. Where's he at?"

Mallory reached deep for all the physical courage he had never found before, grabbed the object off the deck, and leapt up with a wild roar, "AAUURGH!" He swung down hard and buried the hook in Tom's skull. The blow sounded like a crowbar hitting a melon, and a stream of gore gushed out the back of the crushed head. Tom's eyes froze in a glazed stare just before he dropped like a sack of cement.

"Jesus!" Lloyd twitched at the sight of his butchered friend. For a long moment he just gaped, paralyzed by the suddenness, finality, and horror of it. Then he came to his senses and reached for the Colt 10-mm Delta Elite on his hip.

Mallory couldn't believe the vicious results of his own act. For an instant he was stunned by it, but then his adrenaline surged and he wanted to swing again, to erase all threats to his existence. He struggled with the grappling hook to pry it from the mass of jelly and bone, but it was embedded fast in the brain of his victim.

Woody saw Lloyd reach for his gun and reacted on instinct. He lowered his head and charged the man like a little bull, catching him flush in the solar plexus. He felt Lloyd's diaphragm compress and heard his breath rush from his lungs. The sound reminded him of the bellows he often used on the wood-burning cookstove in the communal kitchen. The blow knocked Lloyd back and flipped him over the rail that bordered the stern. He angled head-first into the paddle wheel and lodged there, folded backward over the metal slats, his spine broken.

Mallory had given up on the grappling hook and was prepared for the worst. But he was surprised by Woody's sudden and decisive move on the other man, which saved the situation. With every passing minute the boy continued to impress him.

"Over the side," Woody stage-whispered, and Mallory looked down to see a flat-bottomed boat tethered to the old hull at the water line six feet below.

"How do we . . ."

"Jump!"

Mallory looked over his shoulder and saw several men with torches rushing toward him along the bay-side cat-walk. He turned, took a deep breath, and jumped. He landed hard on the cypress planking but had no idea whether he was injured. There would be time to take stock of that later—he hoped.

Woody was already on board when Mallory landed. He had cut the bowline and was in the back of the boat wrestling with the ancient outboard motor. "Push off." He strained as he frantically jerked on the starter cord. Mallory shoved off, and the fifteen-foot craft drifted out into the stream. He looked around for something constructive to do and finally spotted a banged-up half-paddle lodged under an ammunition box against the right gunwale. He looked up and saw a string of angry men lined up along the lower deck of the paddle wheeler. They were all armed. He jammed the paddle into the water and pulled for his life.

"You're taking us into the bank," Woody yelled.

Mallory looked perplexed then noticed his error and leapt to the opposite side of the boat to correct it.

"Here, take this," Woody said, and a snub-nosed revolver slid across the cypress bottom and came to rest against Mallory's leg. "Paddlin' ain't your game."

Shots popped from the steamboat, and bullets punched the water all about them. Mallory grabbed up the pistol and liked the reassuring weight of it in his hand. It was an odd sensation. He couldn't remember ever having held a hand gun before. He aimed it, cocked it, and jerked the trigger. He couldn't tell whether he had hit anything, but people on the steamboat ducked when he fired.

Woody coiled up for one last mighty tug, then yanked the cord for all he was worth. The old Mercury belched then roared to life. The sudden acceleration almost pitched the boy over the stern, but he managed to grab the cowling and hang on. Then he crouched beside the motor and twisted the throttle wide open. The bow rose as the propeller bit deep into the water.

"Lie down up front," Woody shouted, and Mallory scrambled toward the bow. The fifty-horse whined flat out,

and the weathered john boat settled into a level plane.
Mallory glanced back and saw the wake shining in the
moonlight and the flashes of gunfire that sparked from the
bow of the old steamboat. When they were safely out of
range he sighed and laid his head down upon the cypress
planks. The wood vibrated pleasantly against his skull and
created a soft buzzing sensation that massaged his brain. He
closed his eyes, confident that he was safe in the hands of
this extraordinary boy who piloted the boat. Then he drifted
into unconsciousness and slept the sleep of the saved.

CHAPTER
NINE ─────────────────────────────

Dr. Marguerite Connoly stormed into the Oval Office, slamming the door behind her.

"Please tell me you are *not* sending those Neanderthals on such a sensitive assignment."

"Good afternoon, Maggie. How nice to see you again." President Jeffrey MacGregor believed that all human beings deserved a certain amount of courtesy and respect, so he greeted his chief advisor accordingly. Of course, in Maggie's case it was rather like offering caviar to a pit bull terrier, but it was the thought that counted.

"Why didn't you consult me first?" Maggie leaned over the giant desk, supporting her weight on her knuckles. To MacGregor she looked like a down lineman taking a stance.

"I consult people when I want their opinion, Maggie, not when I already know what it will be. Now what can I do for you?" His uncharacteristic abruptness brought Maggie up short, and she took a step away from the desk.

"Then it was your idea?"

"No. But it was my decision." MacGregor leaned back in

the tall leather chair and propped his knee on the edge of the desk. He wasn't really surprised to see Maggie this afternoon. He knew she had a mole in the White House communications room and usually learned of critical information before he did. "Personally, I think it's a fine idea."

"Oh, you do?"

"Yes, I do."

"And what will you say of your fine idea when those *barbarians* kill the only scientist in the world who knows all aspects of the orbital laser system?" Maggie moved to sit in a straight-backed chair that fronted the desk. "And they *will* kill him, you know."

"I do realize they have an affinity for that sort of thing." MacGregor said. "But in this case, I don't think that would be all bad."

"Not all bad?" Maggie leaned forward. "You mean you would pass up a chance to rebuild Cygnus and give Maximov a taste of his own medicine. My god, he destroyed the Lincoln Memorial!"

"The Russians destroyed the Washington Monument, and we retaliated. Look where that got us."

Maggie leaned back and crossed her legs. She really wasn't half-bad looking in a feisty sort of way. Her legs were good, and her figure trim, and, though pushing forty, her lean face gave her the appearance of someone younger. Her round, rimless spectacles affected that perennial-student look and enhanced the illusion of youth. Her large lavender eyes and full mouth were her most attractive features, which often drew attention away from her primary asset—a mind like a Cray mainframe. "I still think we ought to make the bastard pay. Besides, Maximov is insane. There's no dealing with him. He will kill us if we don't kill him first."

MacGregor flinched. *No wonder they call her Iron Maggie,* he thought. "That's an interesting observation coming from someone who was ready to throw in with Maximov not so very long ago."

Maggie winced. She had recently appeared on national television to plead for the country to stop the Guardians and support a coalition government with Maximov. It was at the height of the Cygnus debacle and was the only time in her life she had ever panicked.

"And the Guardians appear to have pulled that one off pretty well," MacGregor added. "If it hadn't been for them, Maximov and Mallory would have turned the whole world into a microwave oven."

"If indeed they did pull it off, why then is Mallory still alive and well and on the loose?"

"We don't know." It was MacGregor's turn to fidget.

"Why isn't Cygnus still in orbit and under our control and blasting the hell out of Maximov?"

"That will be among the questions I intend to ask Lee Warren when he arrives."

"You do that, Mr. President." Maggie rose to leave. "In the meantime the rest of us will sit back and wait for Billy McKay to fuck up again." She spun toward the door.

"Maggie!" The president's tone was as hard and cold as a diamond drill, and it stopped her before she reached the door. "What you did was treason, and I still don't know why I didn't have you arrested." She turned to face him with a mask of ice. "But I still may," he said.

"That piss-ant little wimp!" Maggie paced furiously back and forth across her office. "How dare he speak to me that way!" She alternately folded then straightened her arms as waves of anger pulsed through her body. Then she stopped and whirled toward her assistant. "He actually threatened to have me arrested!"

"No." Mary Beth Wilson was genuinely shocked. It was unthinkable that the President of the United States would even presume to threaten Marguerite Connoly, the best, the brightest, the strongest. "Chauvinist prick!"

"He is deliberately throwing away the opportunity of a lifetime. If we don't get Mallory on our side, then Maximov certainly will—again!"

"Mallory's alive?"

"Of course he's alive. You don't think Jeff would send McKay and the Misfits out on a wild goose chase, do you?"

"Who?"

"McKay . . . the Guardians. I forgot, you don't have clearance for . . . keep that under your hat." Maggie raced off across the room.

"What will they do, these Guardians?"

"There's only one thing the Guardians know how to do. And that's kill. That's their solution for every problem."

"But the Guardians can't kill Mallory if they can't find him."

"They *already* know where he is." Maggie looked askance at Mary Beth. "They tracked him electronically."

"Within the country?"

"Arkansas or some such place, I don't know. There were map coordinates with the message. But that's beside the point. They are going to kill him wherever the hell he is!"

"But isn't that good?" Mary Beth asked. "I mean, doesn't that mean we no longer have to worry about laser attacks?"

"Yes, Mary Beth, it does." Maggie's tone shifted into condescension. "But it also means we will miss the opportunity to erase Maximov as a threat forever. Don't you see?" She threw her arms up in exasperation and stalked toward the door, collecting her purse and jacket along the

way. "Cancel my appointments for the rest of the afternoon.
I'm going to get drunk!"

Mary Beth cradled the phone with one hand and reached
up to unclasp her earring with the other. In her haste to
make the call she had forgotten to remove the jewelry. She
let the line ring twice, then hung up the receiver. Her phone
buzzed almost at once, and she jerked it off the cradle so
quickly that she almost dropped it.

"Ms. Connoly's office," she said in that crisp, officious
tone so popular among underlings.

"You have news?" It was the silky female voice again,
speaking to her in impeccable French.

"*Oui.*"

"Well, what is it?" The voice was laced with impatience.

"He's alive."

"*Mon dieu!*" the voice gasped.

"And the Guardians have been dispatched to fetch him."

"That, unfortunately, is to be expected. Anything else?"

Mary Beth paused for dramatic effect while she allowed
herself to swell with pride. "We have the location."

"*Magnifique!*" the voice bubbled. "Where is it?"

Mary Beth read off the map coordinates from a notepad.
She had copied the figures earlier from the xeroxed cable,
which Maggie had hidden in her desk drawer.

"You have done well." The voice was a soothing caress.

Mary Beth felt a glow at her very core. "*Merci, made-
moiselle.*"

"You will keep us informed, little sister?"

"*Oui.*"

"*Adieu*, then."

"*Adieu.*" Mary Beth did not hang up the phone immediately. She wanted to savor the moment for as long as
possible, and the receiver was her tactile reminder. She had
struck a blow for the Maggie Connolys of the world whether

Maggie knew it or not. The One Day War never would have happened if her boss and the French woman—she still did not know her name—had been running the world. Well, perhaps with her help, they one day would.

"Maggie will be so proud of me then," she said out loud.

CHAPTER
TEN ─────────────

Fyodor Petrovsky awakened with a start. He had been dreaming of something, something that had made him afraid, but he couldn't quite remember what it was. That was just as well. He had very little experience with fear and what little he had he didn't appreciate. Fear created doubt, and there was no room in his life for doubt.

He would have much preferred dreaming about Natalie and thought it was curious that he had not. Though he harbored no romantic illusions about the woman—she was much too old—he nonetheless couldn't stop thinking about her. He kept conjuring up the image of her ankles hooked around his neck, a move which had threatened to end their lovemaking immediately. But he had managed to hang on and bring her to a peak. He did not think he could have faced her otherwise.

He looked inquisitively toward the seat a few meters to his left and caught the gaze of Kirill Kuragin. His comrade and second-in-command shook his head in reply to Petrovsky's tacit question. No, there had been no message. Of course not, he thought, otherwise they would have awakened him immediately. He wondered how long they would fly above the Atlantic before they learned of their destination.

He picked up the folder he must have dropped when he allowed the drone of the four huge turbofans to lull him to sleep. He looked at his watch. That had been just eleven minutes ago. He studied the photograph that accompanied the dossier and concentrated on the features: short-cropped curly blond hair, cobalt-blue eyes, square face, and a bull neck. He thought he also noticed a slight sneer in the expression. This one was not just tough, Petrovsky thought, he was mean as well, and he wondered if this Lt. William McKay, USMC, enjoyed his work as much as he did.

The leader of the Guardians—*what a name*, he thought, *these Americans are so melodramatic*—was six-foot-three, two hundred twenty-five pounds. Petrovsky noticed that he and McKay weighed the same, though McKay was an inch shorter. They would be evenly matched, he thought, except that the American was thirty-three, nine years older. Petrovsky made a mental note of the advantage.

He smoked cigars—*filthy habit*, Petrovsky thought— preferred old-fashioned women with long legs—*we at least have the legs in common*—and drank beer. He was a drill instructor at the U.S. Marine Corps training facility at Parris Island, SC, was an expert marksman, and had served with distinction in the Southern Mediterranean before the One Day War. He carried a Maremount M60E3 machine gun with a shotgun backup along with a Model 1911 Colt .45 automatic. Petrovsky took special note of the Maremount, judging that the nastiness of the weapon was a reflection of an inherent cruelty in McKay's nature, another point the two held in common. He attended St. Joseph's High School, where he played something called linebacker and where a priest had once labeled him a "degenerate." Petrovsky grew bored. Obviously the man was simply venal and stupid, he concluded, and he slammed the folder shut, creasing the photograph.

Petrovsky had already studied the dossiers on the other three Guardians and had passed them out to the rest of his men. He had saved McKay's for last, revealing his own weakness for melodrama, and was disappointed when the experience proved anticlimactic. Now he had nothing more to do and he began to fidget restlessly.

He looked about the cavernous fuselage of the Ilyushin IL-76 and checked the faces of his men. They appeared as bored as he. Kuragin was reading a dossier; Dimitri Galitsin was engrossed in one of those portable computer games Petrovsky found so infantile; Boros Yakov jiggled his foot in time to music only he could hear through headphones; and Anatole Bolkonsky snored unabashedly, fast asleep. His crew had their individual weaknesses, but it appeared that a hypersusceptibility to stress was not among them.

Of course nerve was a prerequisite for the job, but he had expected some sign of apprehension when he announced their first mission. After all, they had read the impressive dossiers on their adversaries and, worse, had heard all the rumors that had swept the globe the past two years. The Guardians had become gods to half the young boys on the planet. So much so that they could have made a fortune selling replicas of themselves as dolls except that all of the toy factories had been wiped out in the One Day War. But his Serpents had shown not even the slightest trepidation upon learning of their assignment. In fact, Petrovsky thought he detected a certain eagerness.

Perhaps that was because of their background and training. Maximov may be insane, after all, but he is certainly not stupid, and he chose his candidates carefully. They were all Soviets, of course, with the heavy militaristic indoctrination that accompanies that nationality. And, like Petrovsky, they were all chosen from Spetsnaz, the elite special forces of GRU, the intelligence arm of the Red Army, or former Red Army, as was now the case. Petrovsky still had difficulty with that concept.

In addition to their rigorous training as Russian diversionary troops whose physical regimen equaled that of Russia's Olympic athletes, they also endured the fanatical program Maximov had ordered for his Serpent Squad. The result was that he and his men were considered the best of the best.

As Russian soldiers, though, they realized they were lucky even to be alive. Almost the entire Red Army had been decimated by both conventional and nuclear means during the One Day War. But Petrovsky and his men had been part of an anti-VIP company that had parachuted into the Rivers Kaserne NATO installation at Giessen when hostilities broke out. Their job was to terminate key NATO command personnel at the nuclear warhead storage facility there, and they would have, too, except that the stupid pilot had positioned them over their target with an unimaginable degree of accuracy. The result was that they parachuted directly into the installation itself and were immediately captured by security personnel who were waiting for them on the ground. Though Petrovsky had never suffered such embarrassment before, he nonetheless felt a twinge of gratitude for the pilot's error. If not for that bizarre accident he and his men surely now would be dead.

They were repatriated after the war but elected to join the Federated States of Europe instead of returning to a scorched homeland where there was no future for soldiering. Petrovsky and Kuragin then served together during the Effsee occupation of America, at which time they ran an interrogation center in Chicago. Both men were fluent in English and knowledgeable of American slang.

Still bored, Petrovsky checked his AKS-74 rifle for the third time since takeoff. It was just as clean as it had been an hour ago, but he inspected it with great care nonetheless. He thought of McKay as he marveled at the cruelty that had gone into the design of this weapon. The AK-74 was essentially the AKM version of the old Kalashnikov recalibrated for the 5.45 × 39 mm ammunition issued to elite troops of the Soviet Union—before the war, of course. The new cartridge had a slower muzzle velocity than the 7.62 used by the AKM, which meant that it would dump more energy into the target—the human body. Petrovsky had seen some of the wounds the new weapon had inflicted, and they were beautiful in their devastation.

The 74 also offered a new, improved extractor, a new fiberglass reinforced plastic magazine, and a muzzle brake that not only reduced blast and noise but also proved to be the most effective recoil reducer ever produced. And the designers had had the good sense to keep the stamped steel receiver that had made the AKM the most popular assault rifle in the world.

Petrovsky folded the stock of the his S version and ran his fingers the length of the barrel. The movement was like a caress.

"Major!" Petrovsky looked up. Lieutenant Kuragin had appeared out of nowhere with a slip of paper in his outstretched hand. "It's come."

Petrovsky took the paper and unfolded it slowly. One at a time he read the numbers, then read them again: 34 degrees, twenty-five minutes north by ninety-one degrees west. He refolded the paper carefully and handed it to Kuragin. "See that the pilot executes these coordinates immediately," he ordered. He didn't even notice Kuragin snapping to attention before he turned for the flight deck.

For a long moment Petrovsky thought of nothing as he consciously tried to empty his mind. Then he felt the pitch of the giant aircraft as it rolled into its turn. *Arkansas*, he thought, trying to place it on the map of the United States.

It's somewhere around Oklahoma, he seemed to remember, but then he wasn't quite sure where that was either. Oh, well, he would know soon enough. In the meantime he would sleep and gain strength for the mission ahead. He closed his eyes and thought about Natalie and those great long legs. He tried to picture her face, but for some strange reason he could not. Instead, looming in his mind's eye was the creased countenance of a short-haired, bull-necked man named William McKay.

PART
TWO

CHAPTER
ELEVEN ─────────────────────────

"I need to kill somebody soon." Sam Sloan remained strapped into his jumpseat, babbling inanities to himself. But at least he had stopped twitching, McKay thought, looking down through the turret hatch at his friend, who was still unable to manipulate his safety harness.

"First, I want to kill Lee Warren," Sam continued, "then I want kill that son of bitch pilot with my bare hands. And, if it ever looks like I might even consider doing this again, I want somebody to kill me!"

McKay snorted. "Anything you say, Sam." Then he crawled over the side of Mobile One and unfastened the cables securing the APC to the aluminum pallet, which just a few minutes before had acted as a giant surf board. "Unbelievable," he mumbled, remembering.

Unbelievable but true. The drogue chute had extracted the enormous canopies that dragged Mobile One from the belly of the C-130 as if it were a giant baby. The maneuver was like a high-speed, mechanized birthing in mid-air. The pallet hit the water ass-first and pitched forward after one bounce. The package appeared in danger of plunging in at the nose, but the backward motion, speed, and water resistance kept it afloat. The flat bottom of the pallet did the rest, and Mobile One skied to a safe, if sudden, stop.

The operation appeared less clinical from inside the patient. When the chutes had fully inflated and begun their pull, McKay felt as though he had vaporized into a backward blur that accelerated instantly from zero to a million. As he pitched forward and strained against his safety harness, his senses told him he was progressively rocketing down a railroad track, falling off a cliff, bouncing off a trampoline, skimming over rapids, and hitting a brick wall. The opposing G forces he pulled within just seconds threatened to merge his internal organs to the point that he wouldn't have been surprised if he had suddenly shit through his heart.

Tom jettisoned the chutes from the stern while McKay detached the pallet, and after short work, Mobile One floated freely down the murky river.

"Fire this mother up!" Sloan shouted, crawling out of the hatch and into reality. Casey flipped on the electrical system and punched the starter. The V-8 diesel roared to life, sending its exhaust up and to the rear through its new, extended, L-shaped stack. Casey engaged the gears and gradually accelerated. The giant tires rolled through the water like paddle wheels, and Mobile One eased forward toward the middle of the river.

"Well, at least it floats," McKay said.

"Under way, Captain," spouted Casey.

"Very good, Mr. Wilson," Sloan acknowledged. Though Casey drove, it was understood that, with his naval background, Sloan would just naturally take command of the vehicle on the water.

"Mr. McKay?" Sloan ordered. "You and Rogers get below and redistribute the ship's stores. We're listing to starboard."

"Aye, aye, Mr. Bligh," McKay answered. "And if I say 'fuck ye, matey,' is it then the cat-'o-nine for me?"

"Keelhauling," Sloan deadpanned.

"Well, shiver me timbers and fuck me to tears. It's into the hold with me." McKay disappeared through the forward hatch. He and Rogers repositioned the weapons and ammo, which leveled out the vehicle, then Rogers took the watch on deck while Sloan decended into the cockpit to work out their location. He twisted a latch, and a small chart table dropped from the hull. He unfolded a map and, using the LAPES coordinates, checked their position.

"What do you see up there, Tom?" Sloan asked.

"Water, trees, and sky."

Sloan looked at McKay, who returned his blank stare. "Must've been the drop," McKay explained.

"Right," Sloan said. Then he moved toward the hatch. "I'd better take a look."

"Good idea, Cap'n."

There were no visible landmarks, so Sloan shot the sun with a plastic sextant that was part of One's standard equipment. He went below, punched some data into the computerized navigational system, and worked out a position. "Turn her downstream, Casey. Steer a diagonal course between the bluff banks from bend to bend."

"Aye, aye, sir," Casey answered.

"We're about six bends above the mouth of Indian Bay on the White River," Sloan said to everyone. "According to the map, there's a houseboat community up the bay a short distance from there. Maybe we can get some information. Okay?"

"Sounds good to me," McKay groaned as he stretched out on the back bench. "Think I'll get a little shut-eye."

"Tired already, Billy." Sloan gently ribbed him.

"I guess I'm getting too old for this shit," McKay yawned.

"Never."

"Some day," McKay closed his eyes. "And maybe sooner than I think."

A sudden sensation of speed awakened McKay, and he rose from the bench bleary-eyed. "What's goin' on, boys?" He scratched his head.

"Ain't this a trip, Billy?" Casey shouted from the driver's seat. "Of course, it's not as much fun as the LAPES drop, but . . ."

McKay didn't want to be reminded of the LAPES drop. He was, however, curious about the effectiveness of Mobile One as an amphibious vehicle and about this odd acceleration. He climbed through the hatch.

Sloan and Rogers were riding the hull like two beach boys out on a speedboat cruise. The wind stream swept back their hair, and they squinted against the warm sun. "Hi, Billy," Sloan shouted over the noise. "Nice nap?"

"What's the deal here?" McKay yelled.

"We got the Jacuzzis operational," Sloan answered. "Aren't they great?"

"Yeah. How fast are we going?"

"I figure seventeen, maybe eighteen knots. We can do more if we kick in the diesel, too. All four tires, you know?"

"Yeah," McKay answered. He did some quick figuring in his head and came up with almost twenty miles per hour. This was good news. It meant they could get out of trouble at least as fast as they got into it.

"So how does she check out in the water?"

"Better than I thought," Sloan answered. "The new skirts work fine, tight as a drum. And she handles okay on flat water, considering the bulk involved. We won't be doing any fancy cutting, though. You can judge the speed for yourself."

McKay could tell that Sloan was pleased, which was plenty good enough for him. In fact, everything seemed to be working out so far, which meant that something was bound to fuck up, if Murphy's Law still held, and McKay was sure that it did. But then maybe not. Could be that this trip would be easier than the rest. McKay hoped so. The past two years had been chocked full of one insane mission after another, and the cumulative effect was beginning to take its toll. He lowered himself through the hatch en route to the back bench, happy to resume his nap.

Just then: "Kaboom! Whoosh!" An explosion touched off just to the stern of Mobile One, pushing a pillar of water into the air like a geyser.

"Goddammit, I knew it!" McKay leapt out of the hatchway so Tom and Sam could scramble inside. "It was just too good to be true."

Tom dove head-first through the front hatch while Sam dropped through the turret like a fireman.

"What's going on? Did anybody see anything?" Casey didn't know whether to shit or go blind.

"Recoilless rifle from upstream," Tom said matter-of-factly.

"Damn!" McKay lurched for the rear viewport. "A recoilless rifle, you say?"

"Yeah," Sloan confirmed. "And some other weird stuff."

"Weird stuff?" McKay asked.

"What weird stuff?" Casey swiveled his head from side to side in a blur.

"Oh, my god," McKay moaned, his face pressed to the viewport. "This is worse than Alaska."

"Worse than Alaska?" Casey whirled. "That's impossible!"

"Trust me," McKay said.

"When the going gets weird, the weird turn pro." It was a quote that McKay had seen on one of Casey's T-shirts last year, and the phrase jumped into his mind now as he peered out the stern of Mobile One.

"I got one midget submarine and . . ."

"A midget what?" Casey was having trouble with the term.

"You heard me," McKay said. "But here's the best part. I got about twenty retards on wet bikes!"

"What?" Casey was incredulous.

"Goddammit, Casey! Have you gone deaf all of a sudden?"

"I told you it was weird," Sam said.

"Let's kick in the diesel and add a little distance between us and that portable cannon," McKay suggested.

"You got it." Casey started the engine and slammed it into gear. The APC, now under two power sources, lurched forward in the water.

"Tom?" McKay said. "You know what to do."

Sam stood out of the way. Even though it was his ship, so to speak, McKay was still the group leader and always took command in battle.

Another explosion, this one even nearer, erupted in the water.

"Make some tracks, Casey. And while you're at it, make it a little harder to draw a bead on us." Casey turned the wheel, and One spun into a set of evasive maneuvers, cutting didos across the river.

"Careful, Casey," Sloan warned. "She wasn't built for this shit. We don't want to lose her." The vehicle was already riding absurdly low in the water.

"Just till we get out of range of that recoilless," McKay said. "Then we'll just sit and let them come to us. You about ready on that nineteen, Tom?"

"Loaded and ready," Rogers acknowledged.

"Just a little bit further, Case, and we'll have it." The V-450 cut one more swath across the river, then McKay allowed Casey to shut her down. Mobile One settled to a level crawl just out of range of the recoilless and right in the middle of the stream. The turret whined as Tom slowly swiveled the M-19 grenade launcher toward its target.

The sight of the long, low midget sub and the squat, steel V-450 squaring off on a southern river conjured up images of the great ironclad struggles of the Civil War that Sloan had studied at Annapolis. He marveled at how closely this situation resembled the battle between the Monitor and the Merrimac. He just hoped the result wasn't the same.

Suddenly the tiny deck of the sub squirmed with activity. McKay watched through the viewport as a bearded man dropped the recoilless rifle overboard and scrambled for the open hatch. "They see you coming, Tom," McKay smiled.

"Do they?" Rogers asked. "Do you think they'll see this?" He fired the grenade launcher and the baby submarine erupted in a ball of flame.

"Here they come," McKay said. "And what a collection." McKay had fought a bizarre assortment of human refuse in the past two years, but this bunch had championship potential. They appeared to be part bikers and part pirates, if there ever was a distinction between the two. They rode absurdly raked wet bikes, jet skis, wave runners, and powered surfboards flat out and screaming. Their colors consisted of wet suit vests with what appeared to be a replica of the Jolly Roger stenciled across the back. Their hair was long, greasy, and tied back, and their upper bodies were a mosaic of tattoos.

Tom Rogers waited until the crazies got within two hundred yards before he cut loose with the Browning M-2HB .50-caliber machine gun. The hull shook from the pounding of the coaxial weapon, and a deadly spray kicked up just in front of the line of charging wet bikes. "We sure could have used this in Alaska," Rogers grinned.

The attackers ignored the steel curtain that Rogers drew

for them across the river and plunged ahead into the gunfire. One machine exploded under its rider, and another flipped across the water, taking out two more. Then, suddenly, the Browning stopped.

"Anytime, Tom," McKay said.

"It's jammed, Billy." Tom's voice was calm.

"Oh, shit!" McKay yelled. Though he was confident One's armor would stop whatever these looney tunes had to offer, there was still the chance of spalling—a piece of the machine's interior turning into a chunk of shrapnel from an outside hit. There were other concerns, including the fact that he had never fought a goddamn naval battle before. "What do you think, Sam?"

"It's best to keep moving."

"You heard him, Casey. The rest of us'll hit the gun-ports."

A flurry of bullets bounced off the hull as the attackers opened fire.

"Can anybody tell what they've got?" McKay asked.

"I see some Uzis strapped to the handlebars," Tom responded.

"A couple of shotguns, mostly machine pistols," said Sam. "Anything and everything."

Just as the attackers passed on either side of Mobile One, Casey shot the juice to her. To their surprise the V-450 was headed in the same direction they were.

"Let 'em have it, Sam," McKay yelled. Billy's M-60 growled through the gunport while Sam hammered away at them with his Galil SAR. Casey handled the driving, while Tom worked furiously to unjam the M-2HB.

The wet-bikers were stunned to see the amphibious APC accompanying them on their pass. One, who sported a tattoo of a vagina on his bald head, lost power in his turn and floated helplessly while Casey ran him down.

"Pussy!" Wilson sneered, as he crushed the man beneath One's bow.

Another, with an eye patch and a head scarf, fired frantically over his shoulder at the same time as he swung into a long turn. McKay cut him in half with the Maremont, and his bike settled into an idling circle—just a waist and a pair of legs slowly turning in the water on a brainless machine. Seeing this, the remainder of the wet-bikers fled.

McKay watched the water boil a deep red as he tallied up the results. He figured they had killed easily half of the attackers, and the Guardians hadn't suffered a scratch. That's just the way he liked 'em.

He turned to Sloan, who was inserting a fresh clip in his Galil. "Well, Sam, you said you wanted to kill somebody today," and he grinned.

CHAPTER
TWELVE ─────────────────────

Mallory could hardly believe he was standing on the edge of a formal English garden, and in the American South. It was almost as difficult to comprehend as the freshly laundered shirt and pressed slacks he wore or his ability to perceive all of this with a reasonably rested mind. He had slept on crisp sheets the night before, had showered in hot water upon awakening, and had stepped out of the bath to a cup of fresh, hot coffee. The flavor of that first sip created a sensation that bordered on the religious, and Mallory felt as though he had gained a new understanding of the term "born again."

A servant informed him it would be a few minutes before brunch, and perhaps he would like to stroll the grounds in the meantime. So Mallory stood on the soft manicured lawn, basking in the sunshine and feeling the spring breeze brush against his cheek. He could only imagine what delights lay in store for him at brunch, the most civilized of meals. Perhaps eggs Benedict or Sardou or, in keeping with the surroundings, kippers and black pudding. *Fresh eggs*, he thought. *My god, so this is what heaven is like.*

He watched a crew of gardeners trim the ivy that climbed the high brick wall surrounding the estate on three sides. At every corner stood a glassed-in tower, each staffed by an armed guard, and machine-gun implacements dotted the grounds at stretegic intervals. All security positions were carefully camouflaged to blend with the elegant surroundings. The main house was a three-story brick of federal design, and there were garages, barracks, another outbuilding, and a greenhouse within the compound.

The gardens, which lay between the lawn and the wall, virtually shouted with color. There was a blaze of red tulips; there were rows of yellow jonquils, scores of soft pink azaleas, and more, all bordered by stolid green hedges. To Mallory the scene was a visual symphony, and the rich scents of the season made simple breathing a pleasure. God, how he loved spring!

He had no idea what this place was and wasn't entirely sure how he had gotten there. He didn't even know whether he was a prisoner or a guest. He did, however, prefer these surroundings over his previous accommodations and decided the location would be suitable for incarceration, at least until he had time to regroup and devise a way to bring Maximov to his knees and free his daughter. Then he would deal with the Americans—especially McKay!

A tiny bell announced brunch, and Mallory turned toward a patio grouping that overlooked the gardens. He recognized the boy who appeared with a stylish elderly couple. The boy! Of course, it was young Woody who had arranged his escape the night before, or at least he thought it was the night before, and had brought him by boat to this place. So much had happened in the last few days that Mallory was still sorting through a web of disorientation. He had to assume, however, that the older couple were either his hosts or his captors.

"Welcome, Dr. Mallory, to our little enclave." A small,

vigorous man with a manicured mustache and an ascot extended his hand. "I'm Dr. George Ralston, and this is my wife, Marietta."

A plump woman with happy eyes smiled at him. "It's so nice to have visitors, Doctor. Do sit down." Her voice was like a bell.

The greeting plus the boy's presence led Mallory to suspect that he had found sanctuary. It was either that or his new captors were the most civilized and sadistic on the planet—next to Maximov, of course. He sat at the table and unconsciously stuffed a napkin in his collar, grabbed a utensil in each hand, and planted himself before the place setting like a famished version of the American Gothic.

"Hungry, Doctor?" Mrs. Ralston tinkled. "You certainly must have had a time. Woodrow's told us some of it."

Mallory tried to read Woody's scrubbed face for some hint at how much he had told them. The boy's eyes narrowed, and he shook his head slightly to indicate he had not told them everything. Mallory assumed that the part he had left out had contained the killings.

"Hell of a note to ride a fireball back to earth only to be greeted by the prospect of crucifixion, eh, Doctor?" Ralston snorted.

"George!" his wife admonished him.

"Well, hell, Marietta. It's over and done with, and he's safe now. If you can't laugh at these things then they'll drive you crazy. Care for some eggs, Doctor?" The food had arrived.

Mallory didn't have to speak. His eyes virtually salivated over the food and told everyone he was starved. Ralston heaped spoonfuls of scrambled eggs on his plate and followed with generous helpings of some casserole dishes that Mallory didn't recognize. He accepted all the servings eagerly.

"Those are cheese grits, kind of a specialty down here, and that's an asparagus casserole, and those are Oysters Johnny Reb," explained Marietta. "Hope you like them."

Mallory could only grunt in reply, his mouth jammed with food. All the flavors from the various dishes swirled over his palate in a delicious delirium. The grits were a tasty surprise, the oysters spicy and rich, and the asparagus with almond slivers was indescribable. He slugged back a tiny glass of fresh-squeezed orange juice, then lunged for a tumbler of water to wash it all down. Mallory gulped the icy liquid and immediately launched into a coughing fit. For a moment he thought he might choke. Ralston sprang to his aid and hovered behind him, ready to perform the Heimlich maneuver.

"My god, son, don't founder!" Ralston warned, too late.

Mallory waved him away, though he still coughed into his napkin. The fit finally subsided, and the physicist caught his breath. "Please forgive me, but I'm afraid I haven't eaten in some time," he sputtered. It had been almost seventy-two hours since his last, dehydrated meal. "I must appear an awful pig."

"Nonsense, Doctor," Marietta chimed sympathetically. "We quite understand. But there is no need to rush. You can stay here as long as you wish." She reached over and patted his arm maternally.

Mallory relaxed. He knew for certain now that he was not a captive, and a thousand questions began to formulate in his mind. "What place is this?"

"Officially, it is called the Seismic Research Observatory Number Twelve. It's part of the Worldwide Standardized Seismographic Network, or WWSSN. But we like to refer to it simply as Cypress Point," Ralston explained.

"How far did we travel?" Mallory looked at Woody.

"About seven miles by water," the boy said. He pushed

his casserole around on his plate. "You wouldn't happen to have a cheeseburger, would you?" he asked Mrs. Ralston.

"Of course, dear," Marietta said. She called for the servant.

George Ralston noticed the look of apprehension that fell over Mallory's face. "As the crow flies, it's actually less than four miles that separates you from those savages. But as you can see," he made a sweeping gesture with his hand, "we are amply protected here, by both man and nature. The guards and walls protect us from a landward approach, and Big Creek forms a natural boundary to our rear."

Mallory estimated that just over a dozen armed guards ringed the estate, and he wondered if they would truly prove *ample*. "We weren't followed then?"

"I cut the other boats loose before I got to you," Woody explained. "There wasn't any way they could follow us last night, though I suppose they've rounded 'em all up by now."

"And they know of this place?"

"Sure."

"They've attacked twice before," Ralston said, "but we beat them back each time, and gave them a good drubbing, I might add. It's not likely they'll return. But, just in case, I've alerted the security squad to be at the ready."

"Why did you bring me here?"

Woody shrugged. "It's close, safe—and scientific, like you. Besides, I didn't think you'd like camping out on a sandbar."

Mallory winced. He wasn't accustomed to asking stupid questions.

"Woodrow wandered upon us here about two years ago, and we took a particular shine to the boy." Marietta looked at Woody, and Mallory could see that shine in her eyes. "He drifts back into our lives when he takes a notion to, and we fatten him up with food and books for a while until he gets restless and goes off again." She sighed.

"I see." Mallory detected a deep longing in her sigh, and suspected the couple was childless. "I, too, have taken a shine, as you say, to Woodrow. Certainly anyone who saves my life deserves my gratitude and affection."

"It was a brave thing you did, my boy." Ralston raised his glass. "We're proud of you."

"But whatever possessed you to help me, lad?"

"I want to be a scientist like you and Dr. Ralston. Only I want to be a astronomer . . ."

"*An* astronomer, dear," Mrs. Ralston corrected.

Woody made a face. "Yeah, that too."

"So you assumed that since I arrived from the stars I would know all their secrets?"

"Yeah."

"Well, I hate to disappoint you, but actually I know very little about the cosmos. It's laser physics that is my specialty."

Ralston's face knotted in concentration. "Mallory . . . Mallory? You must be John Mallory, then, of Zurich?"

"Of County Cork originally." Mallory's stress meter began to climb.

"About ten years ago I read your monograph on the tuning of free-electron lasers from infrared to ultraviolet. It was very impressive. Tell me, were you able to construct a device that would maintain wavelengths at the high energy end of the spectrum?" Ralston asked.

Mallory was both flattered and stunned. Finally he had found someone in this miserable country who appreciated his work and so might be helpful. But Ralston might also have heard of the Lincoln Memorial and, worse, Vandenberg. Mallory only hoped that standard communications were still as inefficient as when he launched into space.

"You show an unusual grasp of laser physics, Doctor. Is that also your field?"

"Oh, my, no." Ralston chuckled. "This is a seismographic observatory . . ."

"Oh, yes, I had forgotten."

". . . my field is tectonics."

"I beg your pardon?" Mallory had never heard of it.

"Lithospheric dynamics," explained Ralston.

Mallory still appeared perplexed.

"The study of the earth's outer shell."

"Oh." Mallory finally grasped the concept. "As it relates to earthquakes?" *How boring*, he thought.

"Yes, that's the idea." Ralston beamed. "Come, allow me to show you." He started to rise, but his wife stopped him.

"George! Sit down and wait for our guest to finish, please." Marietta's eyes blazed, but her voice flowed like honey. It was the old iron fist in the velvet glove routine, a technique which she had evidently mastered.

Ralston sat down immediately. "I beg your pardon, Doctor. I sometimes get carried away with enthusiasm for my work. You understand."

"Certainly," Mallory mumbled, his mouth full.

"And besides, George, perhaps Dr. Mallory doesn't care to see your laboratory. He might prefer to relax after his meal, or even visit my greenhouse."

"Oh, for god sakes, Marietta. He doesn't want to spend the afternoon ooing and aahing over your damn morning glories."

Mrs. Ralston's eyes narrowed, and Mallory watched her slide the iron fist back into the velvet glove. "George, dear, perhaps Dr. Mallory is unaware of the fact that I happen to have the most comprehensive collection of *Convoluvulaceae* in the country. He might even be excited to learn that my specimens of *Ipomoea violacea* are considered the finest anywhere outside of South America."

"I'm sure he'll be thrilled, dear," George said sarcastically.

Mallory watched this exchange as if it were a tennis match. He swiveled his head back toward Mrs. Ralston just in time to see her nostrils flare and thought it might be a good idea to leap in and ease the tension. "*Ipomoea violecia?* You have Heavenly Blue morning glories?"

"Why yes, Doctor." Mrs. Ralston brightened. "See, George. He does appreciate my work, even if you don't."

Mallory dove back in. "We used to gobble the seeds of the Heavenly Blues during college, then soar like gulls afterward. Did you know that they contain LSD-25?"

"No, Dr. Mallory, I did not." Her smile faded. "And if I had, I'm sure it would not have interested me in the least."

"Oh," Mallory said, wishing he had let the couple rip out each other's throats.

"If you've finished your meal, Doctor?" It was Ralston's turn to leap in. "Perhaps now would be a good time to see the lab."

"I suppose I'm sufficiently foundered," Mallory said, grabbing a muffin as he left the table.

Mrs. Ralston watched Woody gnaw at a cheeseburger while the two men ambled off to the observatory lab.

Mallory accompanied Ralston to an outbuilding that contained the laboratory. There he saw all the sophisticated seismographic equipment, crust analyzers, and computers necessary for the study of earthquake cause and effect. He became less bored as he learned more about the theory of tectonics. Ralston explained the concept through a series of maps that detailed the location of the principal plates around the world. These dozen or so major plates, along with several minor ones, made up the lithosphere, or the earth's outer shell, and interacted with each other at their boundaries. Ralston then dropped an overlay map of the distribution of earthquake epicenters throughout the globe over a map of the plate boundaries. Mallory was astonished to see that the two fit perfectly. He was also amazed to discover that the combined maps formed an unbroken path about the earth. Ralston confirmed that the plate boundaries/epicenters were globally connected: ". . . a virtual string of devastation that snakes its way around the world," Ralston described it.

The snake edge of the gigantic Pacific Plate curled its way from New Zealand up around Australia, and split just east of New Guinea. One branch meandered north, encircling the Philippines, then grew fat over Japan, and crossed the northern Pacific from the Kamchatka Peninsula to southern Alaska. From there it plunged down the Pacific coast all the way to the tip of South America, where it slashed across the southern Atlantic. It formed the lower edge of the South American Plate before it met the boundary of the African Plate at mid-ocean.

The eastern branch of the New Guinea split formed the top of the Australian Plate and wound its way through the Indian Ocean, smothering Indonesia, and piercing the Asian continent at the Burmese-Indian border, where it became the southern edge of the Eurasian Plate. From there it crawled the line of the Himalayas, capped Iran, and entered the Mediterranean where Syria met Turkey. There it became the northern boundary of the African Plate. It ricocheted off southern Greece and Sicily, then thrust into the Atlantic through the Straits of Gibraltar, where it joined the North American Plate just north of the Azores.

There was also the Antarctic Plate, the Nazca Plate off the Pacific coast of South America, the Cocos Plate off the

Pacific coast of Central America, and the Caribbean Plate, all joined at their borders by a web of seismic activity that netted the entire globe.

Mallory noticed that the plate boundaries were either coastal or oceanic in location and wondered why Ralston was stationed almost in the middle of the continent. The scientist switched maps to one of the United States within which was an epicenter and corresponding regional intensity computer projection for all the North American faults.

"We are located here." Ralston pointed to a spot just below an outlined area that included narrow strips on either side of the Mississippi River and stretched from the boot heel of Missouri halfway to the Mississippi border. "That's about eighty-five miles southwest of the southern edge of the New Madrid Fault. The center of the fault lies approximately here, one hundred twenty-two miles northwest of us. Now, compare the intensity factor for an earthquake originating in the New Madrid Fault with one in the more notable San Andreas Fault along the west coast."

Mallory saw immediately that though the San Andreas Fault was larger, the projection of the area of devastation created by a major earthquake along the New Madrid Fault was much greater. The map depicted damage from Louisiana to Wisconsin, from Kansas to Pennsylvania to South Carolina—over five hundred thousand square miles.

"A continental quake, you see, has more force than its coastal equivalent," Ralston explained. "An earthquake that occurred here in 1811 actually reversed the flow of the Mississippi River."

"Fascinating," Mallory said, his mind whirling over the possibilities. "But why is the observatory so far from the fault's center?"

"Oh, my, we have seismographic instruments located throughout the fault, including its center," Ralston said.

"But we chose this position for the laboratory because it allows us to gather accurate readings while providing a certain degree of safety." He appeared embarrassed by his explanation and so quickly added. "There is several million dollars' worth of equipment here, after all."

"Yes, of course," Mallory agreed, realizing the man was an abject coward.

"And then there is the matter of the explosives." It was just a thought that Ralston verbalized, something in passing. But Mallory locked onto the comment like a homing device.

"Explosives?"

Ralston stood over a matrix printer lost in the sheafs of data spit out by one of the lab's computers. "What? . . . Oh, yes. The controlled release charges," he mumbled, then returned to his growing scroll of figures, plots, and projections.

"How interesting." Mallory flattered, only this time he meant it. "Controlled release charges? What's that all about?"

Ralston fidgeted over the material, marking sections of the printout with a red felt-tipped marker. "Hmmm?"

"The charges, Doctor." Mallory flashed a charming smile when he really wanted to grab the old fart by the collar and shake the explanation out of him at once. "What about the charges?"

"The charges? Oh, well, we have placed explosives throughout the fault in order to release any strains that may build up. It's an experimental program to avert major quakes by causing minor ones in advance," explained Ralston. "The theory is sound though there are risks involved."

"Risks?" This is what Mallory most wanted to know.

"Yes, well, possible consequences, anyway," Ralston continued. "An accidental detonation of all the explosives simultaneously could cause not only a devastating quake throughout the New Madrid intensity region but could sufficiently disturb the North American Plate at its borders. This would set off a chain reaction of major seismographic activity throughout the entire lithosphere. Naturally, the results would be catastrophic." Ralston waved a limp hand toward the epicenter maps.

"You mean it could cause a global earthquake?" Mallory tingled with excitement.

"Precisely!" Ralston nodded. "I tried to warn the WWSSN governing board of the implications, but they insisted."

"Insisted on what?"

"Insisted on controlling the detonations from one spot." Ralston pointed to a black computer console in the corner. "There! That's one of the reasons we have such tight security."

Mallory could almost feel his cerebral cortex vibrate as his plan unfolded.

"There are safeguards," Ralston added. "For instance, it's impossible to key-in all the detonation codes at one time, without reprogramming the machine, of course."

"Of course," Mallory concurred, his voice trembling slightly. He wanted to rush out the door and race about the garden like a child, his arms flung outstretched while he sang hosannas to the sky. He now knew there was a way to save his daughter, humble Maximov, build a power base for himself, and kill McKay—all in one stroke. The details were still a bit sketchy, but he could work them out later. He was much too elated for that now.

"If you'll excuse me, Doctor, I'm feeling a bit fagged," Mallory said with as much self-control as he could muster. "I think I'll retire for a bit of a nap."

"Of course, dear boy." Ralston patted him on the back. "You must still be exhausted from your ordeal. Have a good rest, and I'll see you at dinner. We're having leg o' lamb, by the way."

Mallory smiled. *Sanctuary, leg o' lamb, and a plan, all in one day,* he thought. *Perhaps there is a god, after all.* He turned and had to contain himself from skipping through the door.

Mallory's elation lasted only a short time before his brain began to wrestle with questions the answers to which would supply the details of his plot. Could he reprogram the computer himself, or would Ralston have to be coerced to do it? How could he force him? Could the security squad be persuaded to switch its allegiance? Could they be bribed? How many charges were planted throughout the fault? How powerful were they? Where were they placed? How many must be detonated in order to convince his enemies of his newfound power? Would the young President MacGregor succumb? Would Maximov free Emily or say to hell with it? The questions swarmed him like hornets, and he wished he could swat them away.

Suddenly a siren shrieked from behind the cluster of buildings. Mallory heard shouts and saw uniformed men running toward the rear of the grounds. On impulse he followed them. He rounded the corner of the brick mansion and pulled up short near the greenhouse. From this vantage point he had an unobstructed view of the vast green lawn that sloped to the edge of the bayou that formed the back border of the compound. There was no wall there. Only the water and two machine-gun implacements protected this exposed boundary from a flotilla of john boats loaded to the gunwales with crazed men wearing baseball caps and beards and brandishing automatic weapons. The flat-bottomed rigs raced in toward the bank, then veered out in a sweeping turn at the last instant as the whooping maniacs heaved grenades at the shore.

"Whoomp!" An explosion erased one of the sandbagged bunkers and the two soldiers who manned it.

"Jaysus!" Mallory blurted before he fell to the ground. He felt a rush of warm air pass over him. Then came the guttural staccato of machine-gun fire echoing off the water, and one boat went up in flames. A brew of flesh, water, fuel, and blood roiled in the bayou.

Two more grenades exploded, and the other machine-gun nest disappeared in a cloud of dirt and smoke. One security man vaulted over the sandbags like a rag doll and landed in a lifeless heap. His smoking body oozed a thick black liquid that stained the manicured lawn. A fetid stench rushed up the slope with the blast, and Mallory thought he was going to vomit.

"Doctor!" It was Marietta Ralston calling from the door of the greenhouse. "In here," she motioned.

Mallory looked back toward the bayou and saw several john boats slide full speed up onto the bank, their passengers tumbling out upon the lawn like human dice. Unhurt, they came up blazing at the guards with automatic weapons. Mallory recognized one of the men as J. K. Sand, and a clammy coldness shuddered through his body. Then he heard the sickening thud of bullets striking bone and flesh accompanied by the screams of pain. He watched his protectors spin and jerk in the storm of lead and, one by one, fall twitching to the ground. He turned toward the greenhouse and slithered through the door.

"Follow me!" Mrs. Ralston crouched below the plant shelves under the window line and duck-walked to the rear of the structure. Mallory accompanied her to a slant-topped bin in the back corner. She flung open the lid of the miniature dempsey dumpster and emptied some of its contents, slinging garden tools in all directions. Mallory ducked as a rake spun over his head and crashed into a shelf. Suddenly his image of Marietta Ralston changed. He could no longer think of her in terms of an iron fist in a velvet glove. She was all iron now and, with each heave, threatened a transformation into surgical steel. "In here!" She motioned toward the bin.

Mallory climbed into the metal container and scrunched over to make room for Mrs. Ralston. She had gotten one leg over the side when a deafening blast imploded the greenhouse. Shards of glass ripped through the air and slashed the woman instantly into an unrecognizable collection of crimson shreds. A reflexive action flattened Mallory against the side of the bin, his face turned toward Mrs. Ralston. He watched horrified as the slivers of glass sliced through the woman's wrinkled flesh. She stiffened against the unbearable pain, her eyes wide with shock, her mouth gaping in a silent scream. Then she wavered like a battle flag, torn and bloody, and fell over backward, dead before she hit the ground.

The lid crashed down on the bin, and Mallory cringed in the corner, gasping for air and sobbing like a child lost in the dark. He could hear the sound of muffled gunfire popping sporadically about him and the shouts and cries of victors and victims. He could only assume that J. K. and his drug-crazed followers had overrun the compound, and soon all would be lost—and just when the means for the success had leapt out of nowhere like some providential gift. He remembered Dr. Ralston's boast that his security force would be "ample." *Ample, my ass!* Mallory thought. *That insipid little shit!*

Then a terrible silence descended over the compound. As suddenly as the attack had started, it stopped, and Mallory tried to resign himself to the inevitability of his own cruel death. He heard the sound of glass breaking under footfalls and voices calling out orders and replies nearby. Then an unbearable light poured into the bin, and Mallory tried to focus on the backlit figures who hovered over him.

"Well, well, well," came a familiar growl. "If it ain't the good doctor. You ought to be ashamed of yourself runnin' out on our party like that. Especially since you were the guest of honor. That's downright rude, don't you think, boys?" A round of sarcastic confirmations rippled through the crowd of longhairs. "Say, Doctor, can Johnnie come out to play?" A pair of paws reached in, grabbed Mallory, and snatched him out of the container as if he were a rag doll. Mallory dangled in mid-air, those same paws encircling his neck. He fought for breath while his legs flailed two feet above the ground and his eyes stared directly into the face of J. K. Sand.

"Hi there," J.K. said cheerfully. Then he feigned a pout. "I'm disappointed in you." He roared and flung Mallory into a shelf and watched as the doctor bounced into a corner and slid against the metal framework to the ground. "And now, let's pick up where we left off, shall we?" He turned to the side so Mallory could see three men propping up a giant wooden cross just outside the greenhouse frame. "Appropriate for springtime, don't you think?"

Mallory felt dangerously close to passing out and fell over on his side from the dizziness. The horror he had felt his first day back on earth swept over him again, and he closed his eyes and fought to maintain some self-control. He lay there helpless on the broken glass and smelled the blood of Marietta Ralston, which drenched the dirt floor. Finally, he opened his eyes and blinked. A few inches away was a small sign, hand-lettered in script, and stuck in the earth next to a vine that twined up a piece of wooden latticework. He panned up the vine and spotted clusters of blue, purplish, and white flowers surrounded by heart-shaped leaves. The flowers were torn from the glass fragging they had taken, but their seeds were still intact. He blinked again and looked back at the sign. It read, *Ipomoea violacea*—Heavenly Blue Morning Glories.

Mallory raised himself up and fixed J.K. with a mischievous grin. "Tell me, Mr. Sand. How would you like an unlimited supply of LSD?"

CHAPTER
THIRTEEN —————————————————

The Serpent Squad edged up to the top of the bluff overlooking the river. Fyodor Petrovsky motioned for his men to wait behind the crest while he eased ahead to get a better view of the small strip of land that sloped below to the water's edge. There was a house that backed up to the bluff, and a lawn that angled downward to an asphalt drive, which fronted the stream. Crude wooden walkways floating on oil drums were lashed together to form a makeshift dock. Small boats, mostly flat and wooden, tugged at their bowlines in the current. There was an old pickup truck parked on the low bank, but Petrovsky could see no signs of life. He waited, watched, and listened. Nothing.

He had started to signal his men when a sudden staccato ripped through the trees. He dropped to the ground, frantically searching the area for the source of the fire. Then he found it—a woodpecker drumming high up in a pen oak tree. The noise was reminiscent of machine-gun rattle, and *that* was guaranteed to put any soldier flat on his belly. Then from behind he heard muffled snickering from his squad. He shot them a blazing look that brought instant silence.

Normally he encouraged good-humored ribbing among the men as a morale builder, but humor at his expense was something he would not tolerate. He motioned for the Serpents to spread out and form a line, and, together, they descended the hill.

Petrovsky glanced at the garage built into the basement of the house. There was no car. Good. The absence of a vehicle could mean there was no one home but not necessarily. Fuel was still scarce in the rural areas of the world, even America, so not everyone owned a car. Just to make sure, he sent Dimitri Galitsin to peek in the windows while he and the others carefully approached the river. They reached the bank and grouped under the shade of a sycamore tree to wait for their comrade. They had already broken a sweat in the twenty-seven–degree Celsius heat after the four-mile, one-hour walk from the drop zone. It had been just five degrees when they departed Germany the night, or was it the morning, before. With the eight-hour time difference it was easy to get confused.

Galitsin arrived and shook his head silently to indicate he had seen no one in the house. Petrovsky nodded his acknowledgment then sat on his haunches and pulled out a map. He noted that they had arrived at a place called St. Charles on the banks of the White River. He looked at the brownish green water and wondered why they called it the White.

This was the second time Petrovsky had consulted the map. The first, of course, was just after the Serpents had gathered up their chutes and disappeared into the tree line that bordered the oat-field landing zone. The disked plot was too small for an airstrip and so was not spiked like the larger rice fields in the area.

It was a perfect drop, especially from twenty-six thousand feet. He must commend the navigator when he returned, Petrovsky reminded himself, happy that the result had not been the same as at Giessen. Had *that* crew been flying they probably would have landed in the river.

He was sorry that he had had to refuse the IL-76 pilot permission to refuel before they reached the drop zone, but he felt confident the aircraft would be able to hook up with its tanker after the drop, especially considering the absence of load. However, it was imperative that the Serpents land no later than dawn, and if that meant the giant Candide ran out of fuel and crashed, then so be it. After all, Chairman Maximov had been explicit about the mission's priorities. Slip in undetected, he had ordered, and that meant no later than sunrise. Besides, the pilot could always signal the tanker and alter the rendezvous point to a closer position.

They had touched down at exactly 6:20 A.M., CST, four minutes before official sunrise. There had been enough light for the jumpers to steer for the small field but not enough to be easily detected from the ground, especially considering that only the final five hundred feet of the twenty-six thousand–foot leap had occurred under canopy.

So the mission had begun flawlessly—perfect timing, perfect location, and no injuries. Then ill fortune struck. A survey crew and several other men arrived just minutes after the Serpents had managed to scurry from the open field to the tree line. A caravan of five trucks parked within twenty meters of their hiding place and stayed there for four and one-half hours. Most of the men grouped about the trucks, talking. From what Petrovsky could overhear he deduced that two of the men were in a property-line dispute and were surveying the adjoining fields as a consequence. The commander was furious. He cursed the concept of private property and twice considered killing all of the people within view and moving on. But Maximov's instructions kept haunting him, so he waited.

The map showed that St. Charles was ten miles by water northwest of the coordinates radioed from Europe, which was fine with Petrovsky. He wanted to reconnoiter the area then approach the objective from an unanticipated direction. He had had his fill of barging directly into the target.

However, he didn't know where Mallory was now, if indeed he was still alive. The closest reference point to the coordinates was a place called Indian Bay, whatever that was. And, according to the map, it was unapproachable by road. To get there he would have to commandeer a boat, and even better, a guide to supply local information that might prove invaluable later on. That was why he had chosen St. Charles as the place to link up with the river.

Suddenly a heavy thud echoed off the water. "Goddamn shit!" someone cried. Then a figure sprang up in a boat moored under a small floating shed. The floor of the little building had been cut out to make a slip for the boat, and the Serpents simply hadn't seen the man, who apparently had been hunched over in the stern working silently on an outboard motor. "Jesus goddamn Christ!" He danced around in the boat holding his finger, obviously in great pain. He picked up a hammer with his good hand and threw it into the tin siding that shielded the little dock. "Piece of shit!" Then he bent over at the waist in a contortion of agony. Petrovsky smiled slightly and motioned for his men to move.

Bolkonsky remained under the sycamore while the others flanked the shed along the bank. His AGS17 grenade launcher would do little good from close range anyway, except blow up the entire dock and everyone on it, including himself. Yakov crept upstream with his PRM machine gun to anchor their position on the left in case anyone approached down the asphalt road. Galitsin moved silently downstream to cut off the man's escape route in case he decided to dive in the river and make for shore. His H&K close assault shotgun would make short work of that ill-conceived attempt. Petrovsky, backed up by Kuragin, crossed a rickety stage board to a small wooden barge that connected the open slips to the enclosed dock. From there they quietly walked up on the man, who was too preoccupied with his own suffering to notice their approach.

"Good day, sir," Petrovsky said with just a trace of an accent.

The man, who appeared to be in his sixties, swiveled his head without rising to look at the newcomers. He still gripped his smashed finger with his opposite hand. "Not for me it ain't," he groaned. Then he noticed the weapons and stood up. The sight of the two AKS-74s seemed to have a mitigating effect on his pain. "You don't need those guns, boys. There ain't nothing around here worth stealing."

Petrovsky smiled, then motioned to his lieutenant. Kuragin handed his rifle to his commander and stepped down into the boat with the man. He gently took the wounded hand and inspected the damage. Then he reached into his first aid bag and withdrew a tube of triple antibiotic ointment and bandages.

"You boys ain't from around here, are you?" the man said, content to have his finger doctored.

"This is your house?" Petrovsky jerked a thumb over his shoulder.

"That's it," the man replied.

"We are looking for a boat and a guide," the major smiled. "You will do nicely. However, I am not as confident about your boat."

The man looked at his trashed-out craft as if to verify that it indeed was the subject of the conversation. "What, this?" he said. "Why, hell, it'll out run anything on the river."

"Yes, but for how long, grandfather?"

"Longer than you can fuck, sonny boy, and that's for damn sure." He looked at Kuragin as if anticipating some pain in return for the remark, but he got a grin instead.

"But does it run?" Petrovsky's smile faded.

"It will as soon as I can fix the shear pin, and that'll be done if I can hammer *it* in place instead of my goddamn finger."

"Does that mean you are willing to be our guide?"

"Do I have a choice?" He eyed the rifles.

"No."

"In that case, I'm willin'."

"Good." Petrovsky panned the area. "Are there any others here?"

The man looked around. "Do you see anybody else?"

Petrovsky was not accustomed to insolence and wondered how long he would tolerate this man before depositing a bullet in his brain.

"Not just here, but on the river as well. Have others left from this dock today?"

"Oh yeah. Quite a few. But they left out early to run their trotlines, and they're all back by now," the man explained. "And the trouble downstream will most likely keep everybody off the river for the rest of the day."

"Trouble?"

"Oh yeah. Sounded like a goddamn war."

"When was this?"

"Just about an hour ago.

"Where?"

"About three miles down. You could hear it all the way up here. Sound travels on the water, you know."

"Automatic weapons?"

"And bigger stuff."

"Like what?"

"RPGs or some such. I'm not sure what."

"Who was involved?"

"This wild-ass water gang we got down the river attacked a pook turtle."

"Pook turtle?" Petrovsky had never heard the term and wondered if it was some new type of weapon.

"Yeah, you know? One of those ironclad gunboats they used in the Civil War? They kinda looked like a turtle and were designed by some Yankee named Pook. Only this one was much smaller. Armored. At least that's what Tom said. Say where you from, boy?"

Petrovsky hesitated. "Chicago."

"Oh, that explains it."

"There was a witness to the battle, you said?"

"Old Tom Jansen was on the same beach, back up in the willows baitin' his lines, when all hell broke loose. He said that bunch of wet-bikers charged a baby pook turtle."

Pook turtles? Wet-bikers? What strange place is this? Petrovsky wondered. "Describe the machine."

"Well, according to Tom, it rode low in the water, was made out of metal, and had a turret with some sort of cannon and a machine gun on it."

What Petrovsky visualized came dangerously close to the dossier description of the Guardian's armored personnel carrier. But that was impossible because their special Mobile One was not amphibious. Unless, of course, it had been modified. And if that possibility proved correct, then this new information would alter the mission drastically. He decided he would act on the assumption that the Guardians had already arrived, possessed an amphibious APC, and worst of all, had a substantial lead. Even now they could be in Indian Bay with Dr. Mallory. The thought gave him a shudder, and he cursed himself for not killing the greedy bourgeois surveyors back at the drop zone. Petrovsky motioned to his men on the bank, and they scrambled onto the dock.

"Well, I see we got more passengers," the man said,

covering his surprise at the sudden appearance of the others.
"I'm afraid that'll cost you extra."

Petrovsky's smile returned. "The fare for this journey,
grandfather, will be your survival."

"Sounds like a good deal to me. Where're we goin'?"

"A place called Indian Bay. You've heard of it?"

"I know right where it's at." Kuragin finished attending
the wound, and the man examined his new bandage. He
nodded his thanks.

"Good. Then we will leave right away," Petrovsky said.

"I'm afraid I cain't do that, boys. You see, momma's due
back from town here in just a little bit, and she's going to fix
my dinner. You all are welcome, by the way. Then there's
the little matter of the siesta. That lasts about an hour. Then,
I'll be ready to go. We'll still make it to Indian Bay way
before dark. It ain't far."

Petrovsky was too astonished to be amused.

"What is your name, grandfather?"

"Rupert Gaithor."

"Well, Mr. Gaithor, we would prefer to leave now. And
if you don't comply, then I will kill you within the next five
seconds." This time Petrovsky did not smile.

"Hey, fellas, I'm ready to go anytime you are. Just say
the word." Rupert looked into five faces of stone. "Let me
fix this pin, and we're outta here."

Petrovsky nodded to Bolkonsky, and the large man set
down his grenade launcher and lumbered toward the motor.
He took the pin from Rupert, jammed it into place, then
bent it back with his fingers.

Rupert was amazed at the man's strength. "I guess that's
like having a pair of pliers on you all the time."

"Let's go," Petrovsky said, untying the bowline.

Rupert squatted behind the steering wheel, attached to a
homemade wooden console, and pushed against the dock.
The boat glided backward out of the slip, then caught the

current and gained speed. He hit the ignition, and the uncowled Mercury sputtered, then thundered in idle, belching smoke out over the water. Rupert replaced the cowling, pushed forward on the shifter, and opened up the throttle. The old motor purred like a sleeping lion as it propelled the group down the river toward Indian Bay.

CHAPTER
FOURTEEN ──────────────

"Turn up here, Casey." Sam Sloan motioned to his left. "According to the map this is the confluence of the White River and Indian Bay." The ten-ton APC turned slowly and crept into the wide mouth of the stream.

"Confluence? That must be one of those fancy Annapolis words," said William McKay from the back of Mobile One. "What's it mean?"

"It means you're dumber than dirt, Billy."

"Thank you. I'm always trying to improve myself," McKay said, stretching as much of his six-foot, three-inch frame as he could on the too-short bench. He watched as Tom Rogers worked hunched over the jammed feeding device of the Browning M-2HB machine gun. "How's it coming, Tom?"

"It's not." Rogers's tone was flat. "I can't figure it. The feed block, retracting handle, and bolt latch release all check out OK. It's got to be either the feed or holding pawl."

"Keep after it," McKay said. "You'll get it." He didn't seem particularly concerned. Instead he thought of the two suicidal charges the Guardians had repelled within as many days and wondered what the world was coming to. It seemed to him that people everywhere were so crazed with anger and fear since the One Day War that they would openly court sudden death rather than live in desperation on a doomed planet. But at some time during the last two years, he didn't know exactly when, he had decided to change all that. He and his Guardians would make the world safe again, a place where people could love and laugh and build a life for themselves. Maybe even he could do it, too, if he could find a woman kind enough and crazy enough to put up with him. He didn't know if that was possible. He did know that he had seen too much death; a lot of it he had dealt himself. But he also recognized that he was a born soldier, and violence was his stock and trade. It was important for a man to be good at his work, and he knew that at his profession he was the very best. So, like a two-headed monster looming against the sun, the specter of a major dilemma cast a shadow across his life for the first time. It was something he would have to sort out when all this was over. But in the meantime, he had more death to deal.

"We got a fork up ahead, Sam. Which way?" Casey Wilson spoke softly into his throat mike. He couldn't use Mobile One's headset because he was wearing the earphone of his portable stereo instead. He had picked up a local radio station and was jamming to some deep blues as he steered the amphibious monster against the current.

"They've got some great tunes down here. Any of you guys ever heard of Sonny Terry?"

"No," they all said.

"Me either, but he's great." Casey grinned and bobbed his head in time to the harmonica solo. "Which way, Sam?"

Sloan popped up through the turret hatch, then drew back in like a turtle. He consulted the main topo map taped to the

chart table and rubbed his chin. The map showed a false
fork to the left that came to a dead end about half a mile up
the stream. He had started to tell Casey to keep to the right
when . . .

"What the hell! Somebody's cutting in on my station."
Casey turned and made a weird face.

"On your *stereo* headphones?" Sloan asked.

"Yeah."

"Sam, I thought you told me Casey had stopped smoking
that loco weed," McKay said.

"No, really, guys. This is for real. There's somebody
talking on my headset."

The Guardians just looked at one another.

"Who is it?" Sloan asked.

"I'm not sure. Says his name is Generator, or something
like that."

"What's he saying?" This was getting too strange for
McKay. Anyone with an engine part for a name just had to
be trouble.

"I can't make it out. The music's overdubbing it."

"Put on your headsets, everybody," Sam said as he
moved to the communications console. He flicked switches,
pushed buttons, and turned knobs on the sophisticated board
that controlled Mobile One's multimillion-dollar communications system. He got the frequency from Casey, cut into
the signal, and activated the filtering device. Then he piped
it through One's headset network.

"Come in you ugly, stiff-back son of a bitch. This is
Junior Gaithor calling, but you can just think of me as the
angel of death."

"Perfect!" The word echoed through each Guardian's
headset in four-part harmony.

"I don't know about you guys, but this doesn't surprise
me one bit," McKay droned. "This whole trip has been like

a mission to Mars. We're deeper into outer space than we ever were on StarVan."

"I hate to say it, Billy, but I'm beginning to agree with you," Sloan said.

Tom Rogers snorted. It was the closest he had come to a laugh in two years.

"Hey, you down there. Come in. This is your angel callin'," the voice squelched. "I'm fixin' to thrash your ass." A high-pitched, moronic squeal followed the threat.

"Anybody know a gentleman by the name of Junior?" McKay asked. "OK, boys, fess up. Who fucked his wife?"

"Did he say *down there*?" Sloan wanted to know.

"That's exactly what he said," Casey confirmed.

"Tom, scramble up top and see if there is a maniac with wings circling overhead, will you?"

Rogers grimaced, then cautiously pushed his head up through the front hatch. Like a human periscope he swiveled three hundred sixty degrees, then dipped back into the machine.

"I don't see anything."

"OK," McKay said. Then he opened the turret hatch and pushed his massive torso through. There was no sense in asking someone else to do something risky when he could just as easily do it himself. Besides, portions of the horizon were blocked by the turret, so Tom couldn't get a comprehensive view anyway. He sat on the lip of the hatch, sucked in the heavy, humid air, and scoured the sky for something, anything. He found nothing.

"How's the view, Billy?"

"OK so far. Why don't you raise Sky Idiot on the horn and ask him who he is, where he is, and if his parents were brother and sister."

"Will do. Come in, Junior," Sam radioed. "This is Mobile One. Mobile One calling Junior. Come in."

A brief jolt of static came over the headset. Then: "This is Junior calling Mobile One. I got a message for you."

"Mobile One to Junior," Sam replied. "What's the message?"

"Go fuck yourself . . ." Squelch. ". . . Yeeehaaah!"

"What the hell?" Casey turned his face into a question mark.

"Who is this guy?" Sloan begged an answer from no one in particular.

Rogers grunted once.

"Oh, shit!" It was McKay over the headset. "I hope you've got that Browning fixed, Tom, 'cause we're gonna need it." He slid his butt over the edge of the hatch, raised his arms, slipped through the opening, and pulled the hatch cover shut just as a torrent of .223s sprayed the top of the APC.

"Don't tell me." Sloan pushed the air with his palms. "I don't want to know."

"I do," Casey piped.

"No, you don't," McKay said. "Trust me." He thought he saw Rogers smile, but it could have been gas.

"Take that, you sorry sons of bitches . . . hiyiyiyeeee!" Junior screamed over the radio.

"This guy needs some serious counseling," Casey suggested.

"You can each call me a liar," said McKay, "but I swear we just got strafed by a minigun mounted on a dual-wing floatplane."

"Considering the last few days, I'll buy it," Sloan said. "What else has he got?"

"Couldn't tell. I was kinda in a hurry." Then McKay switched to all business. "What's the story on the M-2?"

"No go," Rogers said. "I think I got it narrowed down to the feed pawl, but I'll have to strip it to fix it." He shrugged his apology.

"This hasn't exactly been your mission, has it, Tom?" McKay sneered. The Browning was an integral part of One's weaponry but only if it worked. And McKay cut no slack when it came to the equipment, especially the ordnance.

Casey kicked in the Jacuzzis before McKay had to tell him and jogged to the left in the narrowing stream. "We don't have much room to maneuver here, and the banks are too high to climb."

McKay was afraid of that. With the Browning decommissioned and the M-2 basically ineffective on an airborne target, there was little else they could do but hide under the armor and take evasive action, a term which McKay hated. To him it meant "run for it," pure and simple. But it was better than nothing, which is what it might become if the stream got too slim.

He peered out of the rear viewport just in time to see the bizarre aircraft finish a wide turn over the trees and level off for another strafing pass. The gangling biplane looked even more awkward with bulbous floats protruding from its undercarriage. But even with this hindrance, McKay could tell that the pilot was skillful. After all, he probably had years of experience at flying rice field spray passes, which were essentially the same as strafing runs. He only hoped the difference between a forward strafe and a trailing drop would throw the guy off. And he wouldn't be sorry if the pilot suffered from target fixation or made a mistake with the angle of declension and flew into the water—as long as he didn't hit One, of course.

The minigun was mounted on top of the upper wing, World War I–style, and gave the craft a nostalgic, almost romantic appearance. It reminded McKay of those stories about the Red Baron and the Hat-in-the-Ring Squadron that had so fascinated him as a boy, and he thought how different his reaction was now to the reality. He flinched as the

minigun blazed, forgetting for a moment that the reflection
device of the periscope made a hit virtually impossible.
Still, staring directly into a muzzle flash that could spit four
thousand rounds per minute was a daunting experience. He
had started to turn away when he noticed two brackets
underslung on the wings. He couldn't quite make out what
they were—leftover pieces of equipment from the airplane's
utilitarian days or something more frightening. He could
hold his gaze into the teeth of the machine-gun fire no
longer and finally turned away.

An avalanche of ricochets accompanied the strafing, and
McKay unconsciously ducked. From the sound of the spray
he estimated that the attacker had set the mini's selector
switch to half the weapon's cyclic rate. That meant that, at
two thousand rounds per minute, each five-second pass
would pour one hundred and sixty-six rounds on Mobile
One. It was a good thing they were .223s. A constant
stream of 7.62s or, especially, .50-calibers might cause him
to worry. Still, a stray round that came in perpendicular to
the armor might turn the APC into a submarine, or worse,
kill somebody. He had to think of some way to fight back,
and he had to think of it now.

He had an idea. "Tom, how much does .223 ammo
weigh?" Rogers was the Guardians' resident ballistics
expert.

"Twenty rounds weighs half a pound," he answered
immediately.

"I see." Sam tapped his temple with his forefinger. "So
how much ammo could he possibly carry?"

"Right! Still think I'm dumber than dirt?"

"What kind of plane is it?" Casey asked.

"I don't know exactly. One of those yellow crop dust-
ers."

"A crop duster on floats?" Casey shook his head. "That's

probably an Ag-Cat. Their payload is about three thousand pounds. You figure it out."

"Good god," Sloan said. "That's over one hundred and twenty thousand rounds, Billy, or over seven hundred passes if he's got the selector switch on half-fire. He'll either run out of fuel or get bored before he expends his ammo."

"You think he's carrying a hundred and twenty thousand rounds, Sam?"

"No way," Rogers volunteered. "He'd be lucky if he could get his hands on four thousand rounds at the current market. And he's got the selector switch on full-fire, not half. He's losing a bunch in the water. That's four thousand rounds per minute. I figure he's firing five-second bursts. What do you think, Sam?"

"Right. But that's still three hundred and thirty-plus rounds per strafe, which means he's got twelve passes total." Sam had a head for figures. "No wonder they threw you out of high school, Billy."

Just then another burst erupted over the skin of Mobile One. To the Guardians it felt like a swarm of steel bees had attacked their beloved machine, and they wondered how much more she could take. They flinched and hoped the deranged pilot had flunked geometry—or better yet, never taken it.

"Yo, Guardians!" It was that demonic voice over the headset again. "You let my daddy go, and I'll just pack up my lead and go home. That's a promise. Otherwise I'm going to have to give you a taste of some white phosphorous."

"White phosphorous?" McKay gulped, his worst fears confirmed.

"Rockets!" Rogers declared.

"A crop duster on pontoons armed with a minigun and

rockets!" Sloan was incredulous. "What is this, a Fellini nightmare?"

"Who's Fellini?" McKay asked.

Rogers snorted again. "You don't suppose Charlie Manson got his pilot's license, do you?" Everyone turned and stared at him.

"Who's Charlie Manson?" Casey asked.

"Fuck Fellini *and* Charlie Manson! Who's Daddy?" McKay asked. "Does he think we've got his father down here?" He motioned to Sloan.

"Mobile One calling Junior. Come in, Junior," Sloan blurted into the microphone. "What's all this about your father?"

"You know what I'm talkin' about," the voice replied. "You've kidnapped my daddy, and I want him back. And if you ain't got him, then that means you've killed him, and I'm going to blow your ass to Kingdom Come. Junior out!"

"So much for diplomacy," McKay commented. "Time for a little creative killing." He looked at the others for an idea and got shrugs instead. "Shit!"

"We've got land directly in front," Casey announced. "Looks like we've cut right into a dead end."

Sam groaned. He suddenly remembered he had forgotten to tell Casey about the false fork.

McKay leapt to the periscope and stared at a beautiful cypress-lined crescent dead ahead. The bank was a gradual incline. He was in the process of estimating the distance when Junior lashed the APC with another burst from the minigun. "I figure half a mile, Casey. What do you think?"

"Looks accurate to me."

"Then shoot the juice to her, kid, and let's head for the shade."

Casey showered down on the throttle, and One leapt through the water.

"Anything new on the M-2?" McKay was looking for a Plan B.

"Goddammit, Billy, I'm doing the best I can!" Tom snapped. He had parts strewn all over the vehicle.

"Then forget the machine gun and pan the turret to the rear. If we can't shoot this bastard down, then let's see if we can't scare him to death." McKay had to do something.

The turret whined into position, facing backward. "Here he comes," Tom warned. "Want me to shoot, Billy?" Tom jacked a special antipersonnel frag round into the M-19 grenade launcher.

"Hell yes!"

"This is your last chance, Mobile One," Junior screeched over the headset. "I'm coming in for the kill!"

"We're not going to make land," Casey announced. "There's a wall of cypress knees between us and the bank."

"Dammit!" McKay was beginning to think there was some cosmic conspiracy in effect. "Get as close as you can, Casey. He can't strafe us and pull up in time if we're backed up against the trees."

"You got it."

McKay took up a position at one of the two forward periscopes cut into the turret. He watched the familiar turn, tighter now, over the tree line half a mile downstream as the biplane pitched into position. The stubby yellow Ag-Cat tilted back parallel to the ground and screamed straight for Mobile One. An angry squall from the minigun started up again as the weapon belched fire at its target. McKay watched a perfect hem of death stitch its way through the water and march directly toward what appeared to be his forehead.

"Are you using the timing round?" he mumbled to Rogers.

"Yep."

"What have you got the timer set for?"

"One and a half seconds."

"You're cutting it kind of close, aren't you?"

"You want to fire this damn thing, Billy, or do you want me to do it?"

McKay got the hint and shut up. He felt the stream of .223s rake the hull of the APC and braced for what was coming next. The plane skimmed the water one hundred yards away as Rogers tightened his squeeze on the trigger. McKay held his breath and heard the M-19 fire at the same time as the two wing brackets flared on the Ag-Cat. The grenade exploded in the sky several yards to the right and slightly above the aircraft just as lightning struck the stern of Mobile One. Then things got confused.

"We're hit," McKay announced. "Phosphorous round on the stern." He started to say "Better bail out" but knew it was not necessary. Even before he had finished the thought, Tom had the turret hatch open and all but his feet outside the vehicle. Casey shut down the power plant and scrambled out the driver's hatch, and Sam was right behind him. McKay thought about grabbing a fire extinguisher before he followed Tom out but then remembered there was no point.

A curtain of white smoke shrouded the stern as the Guardians scrambled on deck. Casey and Sam resembled Olympic swimmers on starting blocks while Rogers surveyed the damage from a crouch behind the turret.

"I think it might hold," he estimated, figuring the rocket had missed the fuel tanks, so the chances were at least even the machine would not explode. "Looks like a glancing blow off the engine grate. No fire so far, but the phosphorous has burned through the vents and melted the wiring harness on the diesel."

Casey crawled toward the turret. It was his engine that had taken the brunt, and he wanted to assess the damage personally. "Looks like the super charger's gone, too," he said. "And the PTOs for the Jacuzzis are shot!"

McKay translated all this immediately. The bottom line

was that Mobile One was powerless, both in the water and on land. In an instant the Guardians had lost their transportation, their protection, and their home. "Shit!" McKay spat.

"Look!" It was Casey pointing at the sky. The Ag-Cat slewed into a graceless turn and wobbled back toward the bay. "There's no smoke," he said. "I can't tell if the plane is hit or not."

"Something's hit," McKay said, as he watched the plane stagger in the sky. "It might be Junior, that son of a bitch!"

Then it occurred to everyone that the minigun could still be operational, and Junior might be coming back for the kill. "Get your rifle, Casey," McKay ordered.

Wilson dropped through the forward hatch and grabbed his Remington M-40, returned to the deck, and slipped the weapon out of its case before McKay had even noticed he was gone. Rogers waited for him to return, then went back inside and started handing weapons and ammunition up to Sam.

McKay never took his eyes off the plane, which descended straight for them. "Take him out!" he ordered. His voice was glacial. He watched the aircraft wobble and dip and wondered where it was hit. "What do you think?" he asked Casey.

"A frag could have snapped a cable to the ailerons or maybe the trim tab on the rudder," Casey explained. "Other than that, I can't see any damage. I think it's the pilot who's hit!"

"Let's not take any chances." McKay gnashed his teeth as he watched the stern of Mobile One billow up in smoke.

Casey shoved a 5.56 round into the bolt-action breech.

The Ag-Cat dipped below the tree line, then reappeared as if it had bounced off a trampoline. Then it started down again in a straight line for the wounded APC. "Get ready," McKay said, and Casey took aim. The plane yawed to port, then steadied, then leaned to starboard as it approached within fifty yards of the Guardians. Still the minigun kept silent. "Jesus! You don't think he's going to ram us, do you?" McKay conjectured. Then he, Casey, and Sam hit the deck as the pontoons skimmed just inches over their heads. Astonished, they watched the airplane glide to a liquid landing less than a hundred yards away.

CHAPTER
FIFTEEN ─────────────────────

Petrovsky's slick, closed-lip smile gave him the appearance of a snake. The gods of war were also smiling today, he thought, and they were smiling for the Serpent Squad. He cradled the portable frequency scanner and contemplated his extraordinary luck.

What came over the tiny speaker of the sophisticated unit was a wonderful dialogue of mistaken identity. He heard the voice of a man called Junior, who accused the Guardians of kidnapping his father and was even now destroying their armored unit with his absurd but effective airplane. Petrovsky had caught a glimpse of the machine over the treetops a few minutes ago and almost laughed out loud. But then he heard the chatter of automatic fire and some explosions that shook the countryside, and he suddenly cultivated a deep respect for the comical aircraft.

It was too bad that Rupert Gaithor did not share his amusement. Petrovsky didn't blame him. He, too, would be unhappy if his idiot son had destroyed the only means of his survival, while providing the real kidnappers with the opportunity to surge ahead in the race for Mallory. He conjectured that the Guardians had taken the false fork to the left during the confusion of battle, which allowed the Serpents to pass not only unmolested, but undetected as well. The irony was too sweet for words, so Petrovsky just leaned back, enjoyed the pleasant boat ride, and smiled.

Their guide had become distraught at the events and tried to bolt earlier. But the simple act of discharging one round from the assault shotgun next to his ear had a remarkable effect on his cooperativeness. It did not, however, help his hearing much. Even now Rupert bled from the ear. But Petrovsky imagined the old man would be going deaf soon anyway, so he remained unconcerned.

The old john boat rounded a bend, and a houseboat community appeared on the right bank about half a mile ahead. According to the map, this was Indian Bay. Petrovsky motioned for the boat to pull over to the same bank immediately. Then he ordered Kirill Kuragin to disembark and flank the floating village from the southeast. His Kalashnikov would be perfectly suited for spot shooting, at a variety of ranges, those who might slip through the Serpents' net. Petrovsky didn't want anyone from the settlement left alive to tell anything to anybody. This was a precaution in case Rupert Jr.—he couldn't imagine anyone with that name wanting to pass it on—failed to kill the Guardians. Kuragin disappeared into the woods, and the boat turned slowly upstream.

Petrovsky took in the shabby charm of the little community with a bemused curiosity. He assumed that the odd collection of houseboats, both modern and makeshift, had been assembled by river gypsies of sorts who had banded together for protection. He wondered what kind of people they were and if they would readily reveal Mallory's whereabouts. Time was essential to the mission, and time usually dictated torture where information was concerned. Still, maybe the occupants would cooperate, or better yet,

perhaps Mallory was even here. In that case they would
rendezvous with the recovery plane and be in Germany in
time for breakfast. Maximov would praise him to the point
of embarrassment, Natalie would screw him to the point of
exhaustion, and all would be well. But first things first.
"Pull in here."

Rupert idled alongside of the old steamboat's hull while
Dimitri Galitsin scrambled up and over the side with the
bowline. This was perfect, Petrovsky thought. They could
dock below deck and out of sight. He would place Galitsin
on the upper deck, a vantage point that would allow him to
guard their boat and protect the waterfront escape route
while he also backed up the others with his assault shotgun.
Yakov, with his machine gun, and Bolkonsky, with his
grenade launcher, would help him collect the civilians.
Those two weapons alone would terrify the locals by their
sheer size. So far, so good. Petrovsky smiled.

The Serpents scaled the hull of the steamboat and
dragged Rupert up behind them. They strode confidently
across the wide deck, expecting to encounter someone at
any moment. But no one appeared. Petrovsky wondered if
they had arrived completely undetected.

Finally a woman materialized at the railing on the upper
deck and just stood there, staring at them. Galitsin climbed
the steps and approached her. She looked at him intently,
then reached forward with her hand and stroked the barrel of
his shotgun. Her expression revealed a kind of terrified
longing, and Petrovsky felt himself becoming aroused.
"Bring her down," he ordered.

The woman rejected Galitsin's help and descended the
steps on her own. She approached Petrovsky slowly, as if
with reverence. She seemed fascinated by his black jumpsuit, which, with its epaulets and many pockets, had a
military flair. She knelt at his feet and tentatively touched

his high leather jump boots. Then she rose and took a small petunia from her hair and gently placed it behind his ear.

Rupert roared with laughter.

Petrovsky spun on him with his Kalashnikov and butt-stroked the man across the face. The blow sounded like a boat paddle slapping the water hard, and Rupert collapsed in a heap, unconscious before he hit the ground.

The woman started screaming. She wailed and shrieked uncontrollably as if she were attending a Muslim funeral. Petrovsky was dumbfounded. He wanted to shoot her on the spot, but since she was the only person he had seen from the community, he didn't dare. She might be the only person who knew where Mallory was. He had completely lost control of the situation, and the experience was alien to him. He looked at his men, and they returned his stare blankly. At last, he gripped the woman about the shoulders and shook her like a doll until she finally became silent. Then he asked her very slowly if she knew where Mallory was.

"Sick," she said.

"Where is Dr. Mallory?" Petrovsky repeated the question.

"I won't clean it up," she mewled. "I won't."

"This woman is obviously insane," Petrovsky snapped. He backhanded her across the face. "Are you the only one here? Where is Dr. Mallory?"

"Mallory?" she whimpered. "Who is Mallory?"

Petrovsky was quickly approaching desperation. "Damn!" Then he remembered something and opened the map case slung over his shoulder. He retrieved a photograph of Mallory and displayed it for the woman.

"Crucify!" she pointed. Petrovsky looked at Bolkonsky and Yakov inquisitively. They were all equally perplexed.

"Crucify." She tapped the picture and nodded simultaneously.

"My god, they've nailed the bugger to a cross?" Petrovsky exclaimed. His face fell in disappointment. He had hoped to deliver the man to Maximov alive. "What is your name?" he asked the woman.

"Rachel," she replied.

"Where are the others, Rachel?"

She pointed to the photo again and said, "Cypress Point."

"What?"

"Earthquake Observatory at Cypress Point."

A light shone in Petrovsky's eyes. He quickly got the map out of its case and spread it open. From studying the chart hurriedly during the flight he recalled that there was a special designation marked in blue about four miles southeast of Indian Bay. He remembered all those hours of boredom in the air, then the sudden flurry of frantic planning once the target was announced. He knew from his training that the blue marker was a code for an international scientific facility of some sort, but he hadn't bothered to look it up on the plane. There had been so much to do. Now he flipped the map over and ran his finger down the key index. There it was—WWSSN: Worldwide Standardized Seismographic Network Observatory #12.

"Of course!" he said aloud. Where else would a scientist go but to a scientific facility? How stupid he had been. They would leave the boat and make the trek overland. Four miles was a short distance to travel, and they needed to get the feel of the terrain now that they were in a lowland forest. Besides, the exercise would do them good. It would clear their heads for the action ahead. And they had the time, now that Rupert Jr. had destroyed the Guardians—well, at least detained them. Obviously they didn't know where Mallory was either or they would not have been traveling to Indian Bay.

"Magic seeds?" Rachel extended her hand.

"What?" Petrovsky was preoccupied.

"Seeds from the gods." She offered a handful to the major.

"I already have seeds from the gods," he said, "and I carry them in my loins." He motioned for Galitsin to come down from the upper deck. Then he smiled a becoming smile and touched Rachel tenderly upon her swollen cheek. "Kill them," he ordered.

CHAPTER
SIXTEEN —————————————————————

"I'll never tell you, regardless of what you do to me,"
Dr. Ralston swore. "I am a man of honor!"

"Of course you are, Doctor, and so am I. That is why you
can believe me when I say that I will *not* crucify you if you
give me the computer codes." John Mallory was enjoying
himself. It was rather fun to be on the other end of the cross,
so to speak. He had decided that power was an attractive
commodity, which should go only to those with the intelligence and imagination to wield it properly. And spineless
twits like Ralston should never even consider it. The damn
fool had sat on enough power to rule the world for years and
didn't even know it, much less us it. It was unthinkable.
"Excuse me, Mr. Sand?" he said. "I believe Dr. Ralston
wants to try out your new cross."

"Well, I should hope so," J. K. Sand swelled. "It's our
finest model, after all, with all the latest in deluxe features.
Just step right over here, Dr. Ralston, and we'll help you
take it for a test spin. Boys?"

Three of J.K.'s men grabbed Ralston and gleefully laid

him upon the cross. They were just peaking on the morning
glory acid Mallory had provided for them.

"I'm sure glad it's him and not you on that cross, Dr.
Mallory. I'd hate to think what life would be like without
those fine Heavenly Blues you turned us on to." J.K.
alternately laughed and wept, depending on the visuals his
subconscious sent up to his frontal lobe. "Whoa!" A hand
gesture he had made while speaking left a stream of color in
its wake and caught him by surprise.

Mallory ignored the fool. Anyone who would purposely
blow his brains out on LSD at middle age was undoubtedly
facing a dim future, and he wanted as little to do with the
man as possible. The oaf had wanted to crucify him, after
all, for being responsible for the One Day War. Of course he
had nothing to do with the nuclear exchange and deplored it
as much as anyone. It had been the cause of all his
incredible problems after all.

Before the war he had lived the quiet life of a simple
scientist with his daughter in their comfortable Geneva flat.
But *afterward* he had been kidnapped, launched into space
against his will, forced to perpetrate unspeakable horrors
upon his fellow man, shot, left to die on a platform
programmed for destruction in outer space; he had cata-
pulted to safety in an escape pod at the last instant,
re-entered the atmosphere without a heat shield, and survived all that only to face crucifixion, for Christ's sake!
What kind of life was that?

But now, because of morning glory seeds and the science
of tectonics, he had the opportunity to set things right. As
soon as he got the codes from Ralston, he would reprogram
the computer to set off the appropriate number of charges
sufficient to cause a demonstration earthquake—nothing
elaborate, just a little something to get the world's attention.
Then he would force Chairman Maximov to return his
daughter, after which he would persuade President MacGre-

gor to send him one William McKay for execution. Then he would insist that both leaders give up their power and yield to a higher life form—him. Then he would rule the world the way it was meant to be ruled: with justice, intelligence, and, most importantly, with compassion. But first he had to crucify Dr. Ralston.

"Ah, but for the want of a nail," Mallory quoted.

"Is there a carpenter in the house?" J.K. shouted.

"May God damn you, Mallory, for this despicable deed," cursed Ralston as he strained against the ropes that bound his hands and feet to the cross.

"Oh, I'm sure there are no worries you should be havin' on that score, Dr. Ralston. But then, if you were to be a good fellow and give me the codes, we wouldn't have to concern ourselves with that, now would we?"

"Not on your life." Ralston set his jaw.

"But how about yours?" Mallory winked.

"Never, by god!"

"Then tell him hello for me, will you please." Mallory motioned for the men to begin.

J.K. sank heavily to his knees, placed the spike against Ralston's palm, and raised the heavy maul above his ear. Then he hesitated there, as if in suspended animation, according to Mallory's instructions. The physicist hoped Ralston would relent under the terror of the hesitation, but J.K. simply enjoyed the abject cruelty of the anticipation. Ralston had shut his eyes and mumbled some prayer, so J.K. looked to Mallory for instructions. The physicist shrugged, then nodded, and J.K. brought the hammer down with all the force of his two hundred and seventy pounds.

First there was the ring of steel on steel, then a horrible squishing sound, then a deep thud, then a shrieking wail of unimaginable human pain. A jet of blood shot from Ralston's palm and splattered against J.K.'s face. He growled and hit the spike again, spurred on by the sanguine experience. Ralston's face twisted into mask of agony that contorted and twitched with each blow.

Mallory turned away, sickened by the sight. "For god sakes, man, give me the codes!" But by then Ralston was unconscious. "Wake him," Mallory said.

J.K. doused Ralston with a bucket of water, and the scientist came to, moaning. Then J.K. moved to the other hand and positioned the spike over the heart of the palm, making sure the point just grazed the skin.

"Please. For the love of god, I beg you, no more," Ralston pleaded. "I'll tell you what you want to know." Then he broke down and wept like a child, his tears filled with humiliation and pain.

Mallory took no pleasure in the victory and recanted his accusation that Ralston was spineless. Indeed, he was amazed at the degree of moral courage the man was able to summon and so persuaded himself he had done what he had to do for the sake of his daughter. But there was yet more guilt ahead for Mallory, and he knew it. There was no way he could let Ralston live, and he guessed that J.K. would want to continue the crucifixion. There was actually nothing he could do about it. Without J.K. and his crazed followers, Mallory would have no power base, no drones to do his bidding. He noted the combination to the safe and walked away, leaving Ralston to the mercy of J.K.'s sadistic aberrations.

Mallory opened the small titanium safe bolted to the floor next to the black computer console in the back corner of the observatory. He pulled out a single computer disc and an envelope. He inserted the disc into the machine, and a prompt appeared that read, "Password?" Mallory ripped open the envelope and extracted a single sheet of notepaper upon which was typed the words, "HADES."

How clever, Mallory thought sarcastically. *The god of the underworld. I should have thought of that.* He keyed in the word, and the program scrolled onto the screen. The directions for programming variations of explosions within the New Madrid Fault, including the detonation of all the charges simultaneously, were included. From there it was child's play, especially for one with as extensive a computer background as Mallory.

He was just about to program the last segment when J.K. appeared with Woody in tow. The huge man dragged the boy by the ear into the laboratory. "I got a bone to pick with you two."

"Not now, Sand. We're on the verge of extorting power from the leadership of the entire world," Mallory explained.

"I don't care about that. But I do care about Tom and Lloyd, the two men you killed back at Indian Bay. What have you got to say about that?"

Mallory sighed. "It was necessary evil, like Ralston. If they hadn't been killed, then you would not have your unlimited supply of LSD today." What Mallory did not say was that without the greenhouse, that supply would wither away in a matter of a few days. But he had already collected a supply of seeds, which he intended to hoard and dole out sparingly to only those who obediently served him. Power had its prerequisites, after all.

"You killed Doc Ralston?" Woody asked. His voice seemed to plead with Mallory that it wasn't true.

"No, Woodrow, I did not." Mallory answered him with a straight face. "Mr. Sand, there, is in the process of killing him now."

"You bastard!" Woody squirmed loose and kicked J.K. square in one shin.

"Shit!" the big man screamed and danced about on one leg. "He never did you no good, boy. Don't you see that? All those books on astrology . . ."

"Astronomy," Mallory corrected him.

". . . and other kinds of science was poisoning your mind. That's the kind of stuff that started the war!"

"I don't care!" Woody cried. "It's what I like, and the doctor was the only one who helped me with it."

"I will help you now, Woodrow," Mallory offered.

"Then stop him from killing Dr. Ralston!"

Mallory dropped his eyes and looked away from the boy. "I can't," he whispered.

"Why not?"

"You are too young to understand, now," Mallory evaded. "Someday, when you're older, I'll . . ."

"Bullshit!" Woody screamed and ran out of the door.

Mallory felt a stab of pain as he watched the boy go. "You'd better go after him," he said to J.K. It was more than a suggestion. The fat man hobbled out of the room, and Mallory turned his attention back to the computer.

The program indicated that sixty-two and a half pounds of plastique, roughly the equivalent of one hundred pounds of TNT, made up each of the charges that were set every ten miles along the fault. Mallory decided to detonate just one charge at the northern edge. That should keep Cypress Point as safe as possible at the southern edge and would destroy just one city, which Mallory was amused to discover was called Memphis. Evidently, Mallory assumed, the founder had a penchant for Egyptology. *Well, they will need an archaeologist to discover it after today,* he thought. He keyed in the proper sequence and hit Enter. Then he reached for the telephone.

"Yes, operator. This is a trunk call for the President of the United States, please. John Mallory calling—collect."

CHAPTER
SEVENTEEN ──────────────

"Billy's gone berserk!" Casey yelled. His voice echoed over the still water.

"Just cover me, godammit." McKay, stripped down to his boxer shorts, perched on the edge of Mobile One. "If he looks like he's going to get away or kill me, then drill the son of a bitch." He stuck his USMC-issue Ka-Bar in his teeth and dove into the water.

"What's with the Johnny Weissmuller imitation?" Sam watched McKay swim towards the drifting floatplane.

"Who's Johnny Weissmuller?" Casey asked. He wedged the butt of his Remington M-40 into the angle between his hip and thigh.

"What's McKay up to?" Rogers joined the others on the turret.

"He's going after the plane," Casey said.

"You mean the pilot, don't you?" Sam corrected him.

"You're probably both right," said Tom.

"I've got twenty bucks says he kills the guy," Casey proposed.

"You're on!" Sam snapped.

"I'll take some of that." Rogers joined in.

McKay stroked easily through the water, oblivious to the flurry of sporting activity occurring aboard Mobile One. As with most of his pursuits, McKay tackled this one by switching into his single-minded mode. He would reach the plane two hundred yards away despite its southward drift with the slight breeze. The giant trees that lined the bank baffled most of the wind's power, and McKay knew that if this had been a lake instead of a narrow stream he might have had to swim forever.

He could see most of the pilot's trunk through the canopy of the plane when he swiveled his head back from taking a breath, and it appeared as though the man was slumped over the controls. He detected no movement in the cockpit, though it was difficult to tell with all the motion of his own.

The wind died, and the plane rotated in a listless halfcircle on the smooth, flat water. McKay approached within twenty feet of the craft and switched from a fast crawl to a slow breaststroke. He wanted to catch his breath and muffle the noise of the water at the same time. He reached the port pontoon and hung there for a moment, panting. Not having swum for some time, he had forgotten how demanding the activity can be, especially with a knife between his teeth.

After a few seconds he caught his breath and pulled himself up onto the pontoon. His weight listed the craft hard to port, so he scrambled quickly up onto the wing and up to the Plexiglas-covered cockpit. He flung open the canopy, took the knife from his teeth, grabbed the pilot by the front of his leather flight helmet, and jerked back his head. Then he stared straight into the muzzle of a .45 automatic.

"I'll make you a deal, padnuh. I won't blow your brains out if you won't cut my throat." The pilot winced, showing tobacco-stained teeth. He was obviously hit. "Now you climb down, and I'll climb out, and we'll talk this thang over. Whadaya say?"

"Sounds like a good deal to me," McKay replied, stepping down from the wing to the pontoon. Ordinarily he might have tried a move on a wounded man wielding an uncocked automatic, but he knew this time he had Casey backing him up. He stole a glance toward Mobile One and saw Casey with the Remington shouldered in his direction. He winked at the scope, knowing Casey could see even a slight eye movement through the megapower instrument. He hoped Casey would take his time and literally "scope out" the situation before he pulled the trigger. After all, maybe they could deal with this looney. He decided to step into Casey's line of fire, just to make sure, and hoped he hadn't pissed him off too badly over the last two years.

"So, you're Junior," McKay said.

"That I be," answered the man who moved slowly, carefully, and painfully out of the cockpit. McKay noticed the blood that stained the shoulder of his leather flight jacket. "And who are you?"

"Name's McKay. Lt. William McKay, formerly of the U.S. Marine Corps and presently attached to the Guardians." He hoped the notoriety the group had gained after the publication of their profiles in *Parade* magazine last year would help.

"The who?" Junior said, cocking the .45.

So much for publicity, McKay thought, tensing to move out of Casey's way in an instant if he had to. "The Guardians. We work for the President of the United States."

"Fuck the President of the United States."

And so much for patriotism. McKay was running out of topics.

"Where is my daddy?" Junior leveled the pistol directly at McKay's forehead.

"Before I answer that question, there is something you

should know," McKay said. "There is a rifleman with a variable scope standing on the deck of that vehicle you've been shooting at—right behind me. He can see every move you make, including the one you're making right now. If you shoot me, or even continue to look like your going to shoot me, then he will fire his weapon and a special bullet will explode your head like a melon." He paused to let the information sink in. "Do you understand?"

Junior squinted over McKay's shoulder at the APC two hundred yards away. Then he looked back at McKay. "Hell, I got you hostage."

"The man with the rifle hates my guts." McKay bluffed. "He might shoot me just to get to you."

Junior blinked twice. "Have you got my daddy?"

"No."

Junior thought about it for a moment, then uncocked and lowered the piece. Then he looked over McKay's shoulder. "He's not lowering his rifle." He raised the pistol again.

"He has to keep the rifle up to look through the scope. If you put that .45 away, he won't fire," McKay explained.

Junior looked hard into McKay's eyes, tried to read the lie there but couldn't, so he lowered the gun.

"Now, what's this about your father?"

"A fisherman saw a group of men, like soldiers, take him and his boat round about noon."

McKay arched an eyebrow. "What else do you know about these men?"

"There were five of them, dressed in black, according to old Tom Jansen. That's all I know."

"Did this Jansen fella say anything about how they're armed?"

"Just that one guy looked like he was carrying a cannon. Tom don't know much about weapons," said Junior.

"Where were they going?"

"Down river."

"And you couldn't spot them from the air?"

"I didn't try after I spied your tank over there. Tom said soldiers so I figgered . . ." Junior saw his error and let the explanation trail off. "I was upset!"

"I understand," McKay said sympathetically. "Where do you think they might have gone?"

"Anywhere, but the closest place down river is Indian Bay."

"That's where we're going. Why don't you team up with us and let's see if we can't find your father?"

Just when McKay thought the mission had produced all the weirdness it possible could, another supreme oddity would appear out of nowhere. His current mode of transportation was an example. The ride was like experiencing a hurricane on a machine that was a cross between the Staten Island Ferry and the subway. That's how McKay felt standing on a pontoon behind the wing of the Ag-Cat as it cruised up Indian Bay. Needles of water stung his back, and he hunched against the fuselage for what modicum of protection he could find there. It wasn't much.

The nine-foot Pacific Propeller constant-speed prop powered by the huge Pratt & Whitney nine-cylinder radial engine was the culprit. It fling water bullets off the surface of the bay with impunity. Everyone cowered under the blast.

Everyone except Casey. He of course was having a big time playing in the cockpit of the old Ag-Cat, covered by the protective canopy, while the others suffered. McKay sneaked a look against the spray and spotted that familiar surfer's grin gleaming behind the controls. McKay wished he had found an activity as intoxicating for him as aviation was for Casey. But the only thing he was good at was killing.

Sam and Tom were about as amused by the ride as

McKay. Sam crowded the wing next to Billy, while Rogers
sat on the opposite pontoon holding on to Junior, who lay
out flat. Tom had battle-dressed Junior's frag wound, from
the anitpersonnel charge, before they got under way and
was making sure his patient stayed out of shock, which,
under the present conditions, would be a miracle.

They had transferred their weapons and all the ammunition they could stuff into the aircraft before leaving Mobile
One in the shallows near the end of the false fork off Indian
Bay. They would set up the sat-link when they arrived at the
settlement and order another crew to Hercules in and fix the
disabled APC. It seemed to McKay that the poor behemoth
had been stranded at least once in every puddle between
D.C. and L.A. during the last two years. The machine
seemed to have some sort of aversion to water, and McKay
wondered if it had been a Cat in its former lifetime. He
shook his head several times. The mission must be making
him weird, he thought.

A huge old steamboat rose out of the water as the
floatplane angled around a bend. A menagerie of houseboats clustered about the old paddle wheeler and hugged the
right bank. Casey cut back on the throttle and steered
the plane toward a low dock upon which stood a single
gasoline pump. McKay noticed that there was a distinct lack
of activity about the place. There were no boats coming and
going, no fishermen repairing their nets, no one to be seen
at all. If it had been a settlement on dry land, McKay would
have thought it a ghost town.

"Lock and load, boys," McKay commanded. "Let's
check this place out."

"It looks deserted to me," Casey said, opening the
canopy.

"Maybe and maybe not. Spread out, take it slow, and be
careful," McKay warned.

Rogers helped Junior to the dock, where he propped him

up against the gas pump. There was nothing he could do for him now, so he joined the patrol.

"Sam and I'll take the boats, Tom. You and Casey walk the bank." McKay liked to have a foot soldier accompany the airman and sailor although he knew it was no longer necessary. Still, a little insurance never hurt.

"Will do," Rogers said. He hitched up his Galil SAR and joined Casey on the bank. Wilson had substituted the Ingram .45-caliber for his sniper's rig. The submachine gun with the built-in Sionics supressor was his choice of weapons for close, silent work.

McKay took his shotgun, and Sloan had his Galil, and together they moved quickly from hull to hull. The boats were mostly small and easy to search. Finally they made their way to the giant steamboat.

"Wow, what a beauty," Sam said. He had the same problem with boats that Casey had with aircraft—he couldn't get enough of them. They started at the bow and worked their way back. McKay took the upper level while Sloan combed the main deck. Sam guessed the craft had been a small river workboat, perhaps the last of its kind with a paddle wheel. He searched the saloon and had headed for a closer look at the huge wheel when he stopped.

"Billy!"

McKay had just searched the last of the sleeping quarters on the upper deck when he heard Sloan's cry. The tone was so uncustomarily horrifying that McKay rushed out the rear exit to the staircase. From the upper landing he looked down to see Sam standing over two bodies sprawled on the rear deck. Sloan, who had seen every unimaginable desecration of the human form before, suddenly lurched to the port gunwale and heaved over the side. McKay now had an unobstructed view of the corpses and so could fully appreciate Sam's reaction.

The victims, a man and a woman, had literally had their

heads blown off. There was nothing left of them above the shoulders but scooped-out gourds of occipital bone and shreds of flesh trailing cranium chunks and cephalic gore across the deck. It was as if some sadistic giant had hooked a finger under their chins and ripped upward, scooping out their faces and brainpans through the tops of what were once their heads. McKay felt the bile rise in his throat and fought to keep it down.

"My god!" Tom and Casey had heard the shout and had come running. Rogers came up short at the sight and turned away. He grabbed a tarp slung over a generator and covered the bodies. "My god," he repeated.

Casey just stood there, paralyzed. "Who would do such a thing?"

"Tom, you'd better go get Junior," McKay told him. Rogers nodded and left. "I assume you found nothing on the bank."

"A coupla shacks back in the woods, but no people," Casey said. He stared at the tarpaulin, mesmerized, and just shook his head.

Tom returned with Junior and helped him up the gang-plank to the main deck. Then he lifted the tarp. Junior gulped and covered his eyes.

"Is that man your father?" McKay had to ask.

"Not anymore," the son said, and he lowered his head and wept.

McKay started down the stairway. Something compelled him to comfort the man who just hours before he had wanted to kill. He had descended halfway when a deep shudder rippled through the bank and tore a gash in the earth a foot wide. The massive hull moved under him as if it was riding a sudden large wave, and a section of the bank downstream caved into the bay. A tree fell back in the woods just as the sky erupted with the flights of birds. The houseboats bucked high in the water and slapped into their docks and makeshift moorings. Then, just as suddenly as it had begun, the phenomenon was over, and the only moving vestige of the event was the occasional thudding of boat hulls against one another as they bobbed in the wake of the tremor.

The Guardians stood frozen and just looked at one another for a long moment. An eerie stillness dropped over the woods like a blanket of silence, and McKay could hear himself breathe. Then a howl of rapture broke the quiet.

"Lord God almighty, you have given us a sign. My daddy *lives*!" Junior wailed.

"Perfect," McKay said under his breath. He walked down to the deck and ignored Junior, who had sunk to his knees and was raving on about the hereafter. He sat down on the generator and thought about the day: LAPES drop, wet-bikers, bi-wing floatplanes, a disabled Mobile One, grisly murder, an earthquake, and religious conversion all on one day. Who said the military was boring? he thought.

"Do you hear that?" Casey perked up.

"How can you *not* hear it?" McKay said.

"No, not that," Casey said. "*That*!" He pointed downstream.

Then, between the protestations of faith, McKay heard the faint buzz of an outboard motor. "Somebody shut him up!" he ordered. Then he scrambled to the bayside gunwale. "Let's stay out of sight." He motioned for everyone to drop. He didn't want to lose the only living soul around who might know where Mallory was.

Tom took Junior by the shoulders and explained the importance of his silence. When that didn't do it he drew his knife and placed it under Junior's chin. Then there was instant quiet.

The boat slowed just downstream, then cut out altogether just below the paddle wheeler. The thump of the hulls meeting echoed up from the water and was followed by the sound of someone climbing. The person was just on the other side of the gunwale from McKay, and when he saw a blue-jeaned leg come over the rail, the marine reached up, grabbed the person, and flung him like a sack of cement over onto the deck.

"Ow! Dammit! What's the big idea?"

The Guardians instantly covered their captive at gunpoint. "It's just a boy!" Rogers said.

Woody looked into the four barrels and cowered on the deck. "I didn't do nothin'. Who are you guys, anyway?"

McKay took a chance. "We're the Guardians, son," he said in his deepest voice.

Woody was incredulous. "The Guardians? Wow! Wait'll I tell Mom!"

Across the deck Junior Gaithor shuddered and covered his eyes for a moment. "Woody? It's Junior, from up at St. Charles. Do you remember me?"

"Yeah, Mr. Gaithor. I thought I recognized your plane tied up down at the dock. What you doin' here?"

Junior dropped his eyes, then crossed the deck to the boy. "I came looking for my daddy," he said. There was a long silence. "And I found him." He looked over at the tarp-covered heap. When he put his hands on the boy's shoulders in a gesture of consolation, McKay finally understood.

Oh no, he thought.

Woody became perplexed as he sensed the heaviness in the air. "What's going on?" he asked finally.

"It's your mother, Woody," Junior said softly.

The Guardians alternately groaned and shuffled.

The boy looked at Junior, then at the tarp. "Mom!" he screamed and rushed across the deck. McKay had anticipated this and scooped up the boy before he reached his destination. "No!" he said. "Remember her the way she was."

Woody turned and sank into McKay's huge chest, his whole body shaking with sobs. The stunned marine suddenly found himself comforting a child he didn't even know, and he awkwardly looked to the other Guardians for advice. Their expressions told him that they understood exactly what he felt. So, for all of them, he held this boy as tenderly as if he were the son he somehow knew he would never have.

CHAPTER
EIGHTEEN ──────────────

"An earthquake of all things. How charming, Jeffrey. So where were your Guardians when Mallory was destroying one of your cities?"

President Jeffrey MacGregor sat impassively behind the country's most important desk and simply took what Dr. Marguerite Connoly dished out. And nobody could dish it out like Iron Maggie.

"Correct me if I'm wrong," she said, "but the last time I was in this office did I not tell you that it was a mistake to send those cowboys on such an important mission? Only then I was afraid that they would *kill* Mallory. But now they can't even *find* him!"

"Thank you for reminding me, Maggie," the President said. "But the point is what do we do about this extortion?"

"Are you kidding?" Maggie rose from the chair and paced about the Oval Office. "Give him his daughter, give him asylum, give him the damn pardon, and by all means, give him McKay!"

MacGregor leaned forward on the desk and massaged his

temples. "And when do you suggest I give him the country?"

"He hasn't asked for that."

"But he will. You can count on it. That son of a bitch, calling me *collect* of all things." MacGregor slammed his fist on the desk top.

Connoly smiled at the President's show of indignation. "In that case, throw in a credit card. Then he won't have to call you collect," she said.

"That kind of humor is not helpful, Maggie. Goddammit, you're my chief advisor. Come up with something I can use."

Maggie strolled confidently back to her chair and sat down. "There's nothing we can do, Jeffrey. The simple fact is Mallory's got us by the balls."

Coming from you, MacGregor thought, *that's an appropriate analogy.* "If I give him any of the things he's asked for, then I set myself up for more blackmail down the road. Except for his daughter, of course. I would like to help him there. But I have no power to effect her release."

Maggie uncrossed her attractive legs and leaned forward. "Then come across with what you *do* have the power to give him," she said. "He can't very well hold you responsible for his daughter. Hell, Maximov's got her!"

"Don't you understand, Maggie? We cannot do business with someone like Mallory. He simply can't be trusted."

"He just destroyed Memphis, Jeffrey. He's threatening to destroy much of the planet. Don't you understand? We can't afford *not* to do business with him."

"If only he had given us more time," MacGregor sighed, leaning back in his chair. "Just two hours. We could have a strike force assembled and over there from Fort Bragg in a matter of four. Or for that matter, we could have a couple of F-18s there in a matter of minutes."

"Yes. It's too bad that he's rigged the system so that an

explosion will automatically set it off. And even with a strike force, he could still push the button. That only takes one second," Maggie reminded him. "So even if the Guardians were right there, they still couldn't help you under those circumstances."

"Thank you." He shot her a piercing look, then thought about the Guardians. His Guardians. They could do anything. They'd proved it in the past. If only they could have proved it one more time.

The door burst open, and Dr. Lee Warren hurried in. "Sorry to break in on you like this, Mr. President, but McKay's on the sat-link. Line three."

MacGregor lurched for the speaker phone and punched up the line. "McKay? Where are you?"

There was a slight delay as the signal bounced off the communications satellite. "Hello, Mr. President. We're in a place called Indian Bay in southeast Arkansas."

MacGregor motioned, and Warren walked to a wall, reached up, and pulled down a large map of the United States.

"How far is that from . . . ah . . ." He snapped his fingers at Warren.

"Cypress Point," Warren answered.

"About seven miles by water, sir," McKay answered. "We will deploy there by boat as soon as this conversation is over."

"Then you already know where Mallory is?" MacGregor looked at Maggie.

"Yes, sir. We have a defector from his camp with us now. It appears, sir, that Mallory has gained control of a device that—"

"We already know about the earthquake situation, McKay," the President interrupted. "What you need to know is that Mallory has given us just two hours to meet his demands or he will set off another, much larger tremor. Do you understand?"

After a short delay McKay responded, "Yes, sir."

"Is there anything you can do to stop him?" MacGregor asked.

"We can kill the son of a bitch!" McKay said.

"Jesus Christ!" Connoly flung her hands up in exasperation.

"Is that you, Maggie?" McKay asked. "How're you doin', sweetheart?"

Connoly fumed. "Evidently better than you, McKay."

"Aw, don't be mad, Maggie. What do you say to a quiet dinner when I get back? Just you and me, babe—candlelight, music, the works!"

"In your cave, I presume?" Maggie sneered.

"Billy?" Lee Warren interrupted.

"Oh, hi, Doc," McKay chirped. "Hey, there's somebody here who wants a word with you. Something about a LAPES drop, I think."

"Not now, Billy," Warren snapped. "There are certain things you need to know about what Mallory's up to."

"Oh, you mean about the black computer at the observatory and about the global earthquake and all the death and destruction it will wreak? Yeah, I already know about all that."

"But you don't know that an explosion will trigger the device. You must capture it intact and wait for me to deprogram the system. I'll be leaving shortly. Do you understand?"

"Sure, Doc," McKay said. "Capture, don't destroy. Got it."

"Can you do it in . . ." He looked at his watch. ". . . in an hour and forty-five minutes?"

"Business as usual, Doc." McKay answered.

MacGregor smiled.

Maggie walked over to the desk and leaned down directly in front of the speaker. "Don't fuck it up, McKay!"

"Oh, babe. I love it when you talk dirty."

"You'd better get going, Billy," the President said.

"There's something else, sir. I think Chairman Max has a mole in the White House."

"What?" MacGregor turned ashen.

"Yes, sir. I strongly suspect there's an Effsee commando unit down here just ahead of us. And they certainly didn't find out about Mallory's location from my end."

MacGregor sat down slowly. "My god," he whispered.

"Sir? Are you still there?"

"Yes, McKay," MacGregor said.

"May I suggest you run a careful sweep, just to make sure."

"Of course. Right away."

"Oh, and one other thing. Lee? We got this little problem with Mobile One."

"Not again, Billy." Warren sighed.

"Well, Doc, it's like this. You see we were in this river and . . ."

The heels of her plain business pumps dug into the carpet as Maggie Connoly stomped down the hallway en route to her office on the first floor of the White House. She was enraged. Not only did the President go against her advice and send in the clowns to stop Mallory, but she also had to endure McKay's blatant disrespect in front of Lee Warren and MacGregor. She, the proud possessor of *two* doctorates, was forced to suffer indignity at the hands of an uneducated, uncouth, uncivilized lout. She made up her mind that instant to plan her revenge very carefully.

She arrived at the door to her office and started to storm right in. Instead, she hesitated. The day before she had thrown a tantrum in front of her assistant. It was a display

of temper that was not only unprofessional but also dangerous to her position. And now there was talk of a spy in the
building, so she had to be doubly careful about the security
precautions. She took a deep cleansing breath, just as her
psychiatrist had instructed, and slowly, calmly, turned the
knob on the door to her outer office.

Maggie had opened the door just a few inches when she
heard something that made her hesitate. It was the voice of
her assistant, Mary Beth Wilson, speaking fluent French.
That was odd, Maggie thought. She remembered no mention of a foreign language on Mary Beth's résumé, and that
was something no aspiring government employee would
omit. She decided to listen further.

Mary Beth spoke rapidly but softly, almost in a whisper,
so that it was difficult for Maggie to hear the words. And it
had been many years since she had used the language,
though at one time she had been considered fluent herself.
Gradually it came back to her, and she remembered how
much she had loved the musicality and romance of that
beautiful tongue. Then she went rigid.

"Yes, I know about the earthquake," she heard Mary
Beth say. "There's an emergency meeting in session on that
subject right now . . . Yes, I'll contact you as soon as I
learn more."

Maggie was suddenly furious. Her own assistant was
leaking information to the foreign press, probably some
slick French correspondent who was screwing her on the
side. Then she felt badly about herself. It had obviously
been an error in judgment to hire the young woman in the
first place. Well, she would rectify that mistake immediately. She decided right then that all vestiges of Mary Beth
would be gone by the close of business today. She continued to listen.

"I don't have that information. Connoly's not back from
the meeting, yet," Mary Beth said. "All I know is that Dr.

Mallory contacted the President, and he called an emergency meeting immediately, that's why I contacted you."

My god! Maggie thought. *Surely she's not telling some damn gigolo about Mallory. That's not only classified, that's dangerous information!* Then she heard Mary Beth say something about the Guardians, and Maggie cringed. Her assistant had just given the press the link between the earthquake, Mallory, and the Guardians. That effectively connected the White House to the earthquake and the destruction of an entire American city. By the next morning Jeffrey MacGregor would be able to write off Arkansas, Tennessee, and Missouri during the next election. This was unbelievable. Maggie strained to hear more.

". . . and does Chairman Maximov intend to return the child to Mallory?" Mary Beth asked.

Maximov! Who is she talking . . . what is she . . . why would she be . . . ? When the full weight of the realization hit her, Maggie almost collapsed. Her head swirled like a ferris wheel and she felt as if she was going to be sick. Mary Beth wasn't talking to the press, Maggie now understood. She was talking to someone who had direct access to Maximov. That's why she was speaking French. *My god!* Maggie thought. *What have I done?* Slowly, silently, she closed the door. She turned down the hall and, like a robot, pointed herself in the direction of the office of the Secret Service.

CHAPTER
NINETEEN —————————————

Petrovsky was shocked to see that the observatory was actually a little fortress with high brick walls and guard towers at the corners. He had imagined a pastoral setting consisting of a converted farm or perhaps a more utilitarian layout of government design. He sent Kuragin and Galitsin around each side to reconnoiter the compound while he and the others rested from their ordeal through the woods.

What they had expected to be a pleasant spring walk through an interesting, almost primeval forest, turned out to be an unexpected nightmare. It had taken them twice the anticipated hour-plus to make the trek. Sloughs and creeks swollen with spring runoffs cropped up unmarked at irregular intervals, and the hindering undergrowth was formidable. And all this was *before* the earthquake struck. Afterward the journey became more arduous because of the fallen trees, an increased number of mounds and rises, and actual fissures that formed deep gashes in the ground.

For Petrovsky the earthquake itself bordered on the terrifying. He had never experienced one before and so didn't know what to expect. The sensation created by the very earth moving under his feet was so bizarre that for a moment he thought he was experiencing dizziness and perhaps had become ill. But this was minor compared to how he felt when the trees began to fall. They had been in a stand of deep woods at the time, and many of the trees were ancient. The tremor felled six of the old giants in their immediate area, so the Serpents were kept busy dodging them. When half a dozen hundred-foot trees come crashing down in your direction it will definitely get your attention, Petrovsky thought. It would make a good story to tell at the officers' club back at the castle.

But the delay was not necessarily harmful. Since, as they now knew, they had a small compound to overcome, it was best that they wait until after nightfall to execute the operation. Just before dawn would of course be the best time, for a variety of reasons, not the least of which was that the following daylight would be required for rendezvousing with the recovery aircraft. They would sneak in, collect Mallory, shoot their way out if necessary, and make for the landing strip located in an unspiked field less than ten miles away. If they could secure a boat, that would be even better since the field was located near the river. But it did not matter. None of Petrovsky's men expected to live if wounded anyway.

When Galitsin returned with the portable power booster for the radio, he would contact the communications aircraft that even now hovered over the Atlantic. The sophisticated equipment aboard would relay the signal to Europe, and he could get the latest intelligence on the Guardians. However, Petrovsky was sure they were either dead or drastically delayed because of their encounter with the crop duster. *Think of it,* he mused. *The great Guardians done in by a biplane.*

And even if they did survive the aerial attack and made it to Indian Bay, there was no one there to point them in the

right direction. Galitsin had seen to that with his combat
shotgun. Petrovsky had watched him place the muzzle
underneath the woman's chin and click the selector switch
to full-auto. The weapon fired at least three rounds before
Galitsin could release the trigger.

Even if there had been anyone to tell them of Mallory's
location, they had no boat and would have to negotiate the
same path as the Serpents—but at night. Petrovsky shuddered to think what that journey would be like in the dark.
He was glad he had ordered Yakov to scuttle Rupert's boat.

The scouts returned, and Petrovsky heard their reports.
He laughed when he learned that the opposition was made
up mostly of undisciplined civilians, middle-aged drug
addicts, and a few wounded security soldiers. There were a
lot of them, however, more than fifty people in the
compound counting women and children.

He took Galitsin's report first, then ordered him to
contact the communications ship. He was dissappointed to
hear there was no message from Europe on the condition
and whereabouts of the Guardians. He felt sure that they
would have communicated their ill fortune to Washington,
and Natalie's asset would have passed on the information by
now. The silence meant either that their communications
equipment had been destroyed or that they had all been
killed. Petrovsky somehow doubted the latter. He couldn't
explain it, but he somehow felt the impending presence of
Lt. William McKay. He shuddered once and the feeling
went away.

Petrovsky formulated the plan of attack, discussed it with
Kuragin, as he always did, and issued the orders to the
others. He would place Bolkonsky with the grenade
launcher at the front gate. The structure was of solid iron,
but the center lock mechanism was vulnerable to a shaped
charge of white phosphorous. He had hopes, however, that
Yakov and Galitsin could each silently take out the tower

guards at either end of the front wall, converge on the gate, and open it from the inside. Then he, Kuragin, and Bolkonsky could simply walk through. From there they would fan out and search for Mallory, since they had no intelligence on the compound's interior other than what Kuragin and Galitsin were able to see on their reconnaissance. He and Kuragin would take the main house because that's where they expected the doctor to be. If they encountered any opposition, they would use their knives and suppressed pistols to perpetuate the silence of the attack.

With the reconnaissance performed and plans devised, the Serpents settled into the undergrowth for the night. The light would be gone in another half hour, and they could move around a bit more freely, though Petrovsky doubted they would want to. They were in excellent shape, but his men had been through a lot today. And the earthquake had proved unnerving.

He watched them as they sprawled on the ground, resting, cleaning weapons, thinking. There was Kuragin, his steady right hand; Bulkonsky, the quiet giant; Galitsin, the killer; and Yakov, the clown. He liked and respected them all, but especially Kuragin and Yakov.

It was Boros Yakov who had kept them entertained during the months of grueling training. He had exceptionally keen hearing for a sighted man and could detect approaching vehicles long before anyone else in the group. He liked to display this ability through a little trick where he would look in one direction and point in another until, minutes later, a car or plane or boat would appear exactly where he pointed. Petrovsky noticed that he was performing that trick now. And his finger was pointed at the sky.

Almost a full five minutes later Petrovsky saw the aircraft. It was the same bizarre double-winged floatplane that had attacked the Guardians earlier that afternoon.

Good, Petrovsky thought. The very presence of the plane means that it must have destroyed the Guardians. That confirmed the lack of intelligence out of Washington. He watched the plane circle overhead for several minutes before it finally flew away. He settled back in the grass and closed his eyes, confident that his Serpents would perform the extraction operation almost unopposed.

CHAPTER
TWENTY ———————————

The old Ag-Cat lurched and sputtered as Casey worked the throttle to the huge radial engine on his approach to the lower end of Big Creek. He had plenty of room to set it down in the wide bend where the stream joined the White River a mile below the mouth of Indian Bay. Both pontoons skimmed the drab surface simultaneously, and the plane settled into a perfect landing.

McKay marveled at Casey's skill. He didn't know whether Wilson had ever earned his water wings, but he knew for a fact that he hadn't flown a seaplane in a *long* time. Yet he had just executed the difficult maneuver flawlessly.

Casey taxied toward the bank and cut the engine at just the right time so the craft coasted slowly to the moored john boat. Sloan and Rogers rose to brace each wing, and the old machine came to a graceful stop. Woody tended the outboard while Junior, still weak from his wound, stretched out on the cypress planks. Casey bounded out of the cockpit and into the boat to brief McKay while Sam and Tom tied up the plane.

"What did you see up there, hotshot?"

"Well, I found the compound all right. No trouble there. It's only about a mile upstream," Casey said. "The layout is exactly like the boy described it. He's got a good eye for detail, by the way. We might want to recruit him later on.

"Anyway, the place is trashed—the aftermath of the attack, I suppose. And there are women and children and longhairs everywhere. I estimate thirty-five or forty, not counting those indoors.

"The security precautions look pretty lax, though the obstacles are just like Woody said: a wall on three sides about ten feet high, towers at the corners manned by one guard each, I think. Two obvious machine-gun locations in the back guarding the water—sandbagged nests, been worked over pretty good—and one other I just happened to spot hidden in the foliage. I suspect there are others like it hidden elsewhere, but I couldn't tell. None of these implacements were manned, believe it or not, except for the guard towers. That's about it."

"No sign of anyone else?" McKay cocked his head.

"You mean like a commando group?" Casey asked. "No, but then I doubt I would have seen them, anyway, Billy. You know that."

"Yeah, right."

"Oh, there was one other thing," Casey said. "In the middle of a long lawn that slopes down to the water in the rear of the place, there was this big cross . . ."

"Not another religious group. "McKay sighed, remembering all the trouble those fanatics from the Church of the New Dispensation had given him in the past.

"I don't think so," answered Casey. "This cross had a man nailed to it!"

"Jesus!" McKay was freaked.

"No, but there were some similarities."

McKay groaned.

"So what's the plan?" Casey asked.

McKay looked at his watch. "Well, we've got thirty-two minutes until the deadline and a little less than that till sundown. Too bad we can't use the plane, by the way, but I guess it's not really our style to strafe women and children."

"I don't think the editors at *Parade* would like it much," Casey deadpanned.

"I don't either," Sam agreed. He and Tom had just returned from tying up the Ag-Cat.

McKay looked up. "Let's go in from the water side, boys. We'll split up. I'll go for the lab that houses the computer. Chances are Mallory will be there. If not, you and Tom can search the mansion for him, Casey. Sam, you take one of the machine-gun nests down by the slough and hold it for covering fire and backup. Any questions?"

Sloan and Rogers shook their heads. They remembered the layout from Woody's descriptions and understood from the conversation that it was accurate.

"All right, let's saddle up," McKay barked. "Get your gear together. Woody, take her upstream, slow."

The boy cranked up the old forty-horse Johnson, turned the boat into the current, and crept along the bank. A half mile later he cut the engine, and the cypress hull glided silently into the willows.

"Junior, you and Woody stay with the boat," McKay whispered through teeth that stood out like pearls against his blackened face. "We might need it later." He gave his gear a final check: the M-60 with five clips, six grenades—three frags and three stuns—the Colt .45 and three clips, and his Ka-Bar sheathed upside-down on his breast. He figured if he needed any more than that he was in the wrong business. The others were just finishing up with their cammo night cream. "All right, Guardians," McKay rasped. "Let's go to work." And they slipped over the side and disappeared into the growing darkness.

Petrovsky sat alone in the dusk with his back against a tree while the others prepared their gear. He had just received a communication from Europe, a patch-through from Maximov himself. What he learned had astounded him.

Mallory himself had caused the earthquake and was threatening another that would shake the world. He had also forced Maximov to relinquish his daughter—not an easy feat, Petrovsky imagined. This Mallory had turned out to be more formidable than he had thought, despite Maximov's original description of him as an "ineffectual egghead."

He had also learned that the scientist had set a deadline that would expire in—Petrovsky glanced at his watch—nineteen minutes. That left no time for his original concept of attack, so he would have to go with Plan B—blast open the damn gate and rush the place, hoping to beat Mallory to the computer, wherever that was. *Shit!* he thought.

Maximov also informed him that their asset in Washington had been discovered. When they had tried to contact her, Maximov related, they were informed by a receptionist that she no longer was employed at the White House. So the implications drawn earlier from the absence of intelligence had gone from extremely positive to about as bad as they could get. With one exception. There was still no word on the Guardians, so they might yet be lying dead in the false fork of Indian Bay—there was the appearance of the plane, after all. Still, the creased image of the short-haired man with the cruel sneer loomed in Petrovsky's mind.

The consequences of all of these developments were that Maximov had dispatched the rendezvous plane and had ordered the Serpents to attack immediately. So, that was that.

Oh, yes, Petrovsky had almost forgotten. There was one other thing. After he had wished him good fortune, Maximov politely reminded Petrovsky that he need not return if he failed.

John Mallory whistled "Londonderry Air" as he stepped out on the front porch of the mansion and drank in the spectacle of the warm, scented night. The aromas from the garden provided invisible delights that rivaled the brilliant, diamond-lit sky. He looked up at the sea of stars and thought of his recent voyage among them and of all he had come through to finally arrive at his moment of glory. He also thought of young Woody and lamented his absence. Without the boy, Mallory knew, he would now be dead and all would have been lost—his new power, his daughter's freedom, everything. *What a a lad*, he thought.

He had just received a phone call from Liam Malone in Belfast. Emily had touched down there just moments before and was now safe under a blanket of IRA security. Not even Maximov dared to brook their authority, at least in Northern Ireland. As a grandson of a martyred freedom fighter, Mallory called in a debt of honor on the organization of which his old school chum was now the leader. *Thank God for my grandfather*, Mallory thought.

He walked down the steps, turned toward the laboratory, and contemplated the progress of his plan. The earthquake had gone smoothly enough, though it had been a tad stronger than he had anticipated—knocking down trees and such. He was also genuinely sorry about the tragic outcome in Memphis, but casualties were inevitable during a revolution, even if it was just a one-man operation. They would rebuild the city in time and forget all about today's little incident.

There was just one other loose end, however. He still had not heard from MacGregor in Washington. He assumed that the President was holding out until the last minute as a face-saving gesture. Well, Mallory could appreciate that and would allow the young politician his last little display of theatrics. However, if McKay did not appear at his gate by the deadline in just—he look at his wristwatch—fourteen minutes, he would have to punish MacGregor's disobedience with another little jolt to the lithosphere.

He walked around the house and down the back lawn toward the stream, or slough, as it was called here. He tried to ignore the huge cross that loomed up against the sparkling sky but could not. It was ghastly, he thought, as he patted his lamb-filled belly and gave thanks that it was Ralston instead of him who hung there.

He ambled over toward the lab, which also housed the compound's communication gear. Perhaps a message had arrived from MacGregor since he had stepped out, he speculated, and he decided to check and see. But just as he finished his thought a deafening explosion rocked the night. It came from the front gate. Mallory looked at the light shining through the window of the lab and thought of Emily. "Jaysus!" he cried, and ran for the light.

McKay crawled out of the slough on his belly and tried to be as quiet about it as possible. He caught his breath and looked about for the inevitable sentry. He spotted him about fifteen yards to his left and gulped at the proximity. He blessed the United States Marine Corps and Major Crenna for his training, then drew his knife and, like a panther in the night, crept up behind the unsuspecting guard and buried his Ka-Bar up to the hilt in his side. He felt the carbon steel point pierce the liver, and the shock and pain stifled any cry the man may have contemplated.

The other Guardians, dripping wet, gathered around their leader and admired his handiwork.

"Nicely done, Billy," Rogers said. "Not a sound."

"Where's the lab?" McKay whispered.

"To the left according to Woody," Sam responded.

"He's been right so far," McKay said. "Casey, Tom, there's the mansion. You know what to do. Be careful."

The two slunk off toward the large brick house and vanished in the darkness. Sam crawled into an unattended circle of sandbags and bumped his head on an ammunition case. McKay heard his whispered "Shit" halfway across the lawn.

Then an explosion erupted from the opposite side of the house. McKay flung himself to the ground and tried to hide behind a blade of grass as searchlights lit up the night.

"Perfect," he said out loud.

The rest of the Serpents were crouched behind a huge tree trunk when Bolkonsky blew the gate. They bolted from around their shield and rushed through the opening with their weapons blazing. Petrovsky saw the glass of one tower shatter when Yakov hosed it with his PRM machine gun. The 9-mm spray propelled a hapless guard out of the tower and over the wall. The other tower simply disintegrated from the blast of Bolkonsky's 30-mm AGS17 grenade launcher. Petrovsky never saw its occupant, who he assumed had vaporized in a sheet of steel.

He motioned for Galitsin, Yakov, and Bolkonsky to storm the main house while he and Kuragin searched the outbuildings and grounds for the computer.

A shaggy-haired man in blue jeans and no shirt appeared on the front porch with a machine pistol. His gunfire forced the Serpents to the ground until Yakov cut the man down. "Foolish amateur," Petrovsky said out loud.

They got up and rushed through the garden, seeking cover more substantial than flowers and shrubs. They had made it to within twenty meters of the house when a hail of .50-caliber fire sent them sprawling. A machine-gun implacement hidden along the right wall held command of the entire garden and nailed the squad to the ground. Petrovsky bit into the earth and counted the precious seconds while bullets kicked up tiny tornados all around him.

Finally Bolkonsky got off a round that silenced the .50-caliber in a cloud of fragmentation. Then all of the Serpents bolted simultaneously for the safety of the house. Being pinned down in the open once was enough for all of them.

They reached the porch, and Galitsin, Yakov, and Bolkonsky swept through the front door while Petrovsky and Kuragin edged along the exterior wall of the house and disappeared around the corner. They had covered less than five meters when a single shot caught Kuragin in the base of his spine and bent him backward. He writhed from the waist up, but his dead legs lay motionless on the ground. He looked up at Petrovsky with a sad-eyed smile and moaned, "Do it!" His major pointed the Kalashnikov behind Kuragin's ear and flipped the selector switch to Single Shot. He said, "Close your eyes, old comrade, and sleep well," and he pulled the trigger.

McKay looked to his left and, over the charred sandbags, saw Sloan pop the ammo case, touch the bump on his head, curse, and lay out the belts for the old M-73 machine gun. He knew Sam could use a loader, but since no one volunteered, the naval commander would just have to perform double duty. When McKay saw Sloan track the belt into the link feeder and cock the weapon, he gave him the high sign and broke for what he hoped was the lab.

Several men who moved as if they had suffered various degrees of brain damage poured out of a side door of the main house and onto the expansive screened veranda. They were all armed with automatic weapons, and the unbroken stream of muzzle flashing indicated that their selector switches were on full. McKay did his Pete Rose imitation and dove into a head-slide as bullets kicked up pieces of lawn all around him. Then he heard a deep growling chatter to his rear and knew that Sam had come to his rescue.

The .50-caliber slugs ripped through the posts, screening, and waist board of the porch like an invisible chain saw on speed. The shooters on the porch spun and tumbled under the withering fire. One enormous redneck, who looked like a bear, twitched backward into the rear wall of the house, bounced forward the full breadth of the porch, and flipped over the waist board into a bed of azaleas, collecting lead every lurching step of the way. McKay figured the man weighed two-seventy before he got shot and about three-twenty-five afterward.

Sloan's cover with the M-73 did the job, and the gunfire from the porch subsided. McKay looked toward a low building he thought was the lab and saw a shadowed figure with white hair scurry through the door. He grabbed his M-60 and bolted in the same direction.

The spectacle filled Woody with wonderment. He sat in the stern of the boat awestruck by the booming explosions, the chattering gunfire, the plumes of flame, and the strobe effect of the small-arms fire in the darkness.

"I cain't stand it no longer," Junior said from the bow. "I can feel that my daddy's killers are in there, and vengeance is *mine!*" He got out of the boat and, holding his shoulder, pivoted toward the battle. Then he stopped, turned, and walked back to Woody. He reached inside his leather flight jacket and withdrew an old Browning Challenger II .22 automatic pistol. "My daddy give it to me. Just pull this back," he pointed to the breech, "and push this down," he demonstrated the thumb safety, "and she's ready to fire. The clip holds thirteen shots."

"What are you gonna use?" Woody asked, taking the heavy piece in his hand.

"God will provide," Junior said with enough conviction to make the boy believe it. Then he turned and walked up the bank.

Tom and Casey moved cautiously through the kitchen, their backs to one another, facing outward. A man in a baseball cap and cowboy shirt and holding an AK-47 stepped into the room. Casey saw him first and let go with a measured burst from his Ingram. The .45 slugs twirled the man in a half circle and flung him against the wall. His back smeared the wallpaper with blood as he slid to the floor.

They rounded the corner and crept into the dining room. The huge table was heaped with food, and if Casey hadn't been just slightly more wary than hungry, he would have called a halt to the proceedings right then and paused for a dinner break. Maybe later, he thought.

Suddenly a huge figure dressed in black appeared in the alcove entrance. Tom and Casey simultaneously recognized the giant's weapon and dove for the kitchen doorway. They felt the concussion of the "whomp" and heard the fragments rip into the walls. Rogers crawled along the kitchen floor to the door and peeked around the corner. He was able to make out two stumps for legs through the dust and smoke. He retreated beyond the jam, drew his Browning automatic, crawled back to the doorway, and shot the man once in each knee. The giant bellowed in pain and jerked the trigger of his grenade launcher in reflex. The room erupted in steel and smoke.

Tom and Casey decided it was best to keep low, so they crawled in the other direction, into the pantry. Casey rose with his back to the wall and slid around the corner into a large sitting room. There, two other men in black let go with a spray of automatic fire that stitched Casey up the right shoulder. He sucked in a cry and collapsed.

Rogers heard the gunfire and accompanying gasp and crawled around the corner. He could see Casey's young eyes start to glaze over in shock. He also saw the two pairs of feet step in his direction. He leapt up from the floor and zipped off a full clip at the two men, who never saw him coming. Both flew backward across the room. The one on the left held a huge machine gun pointed up, which he fired continuously into the ceiling as he fell.

Mallory entered the lab gasping for air. He rushed over to the safe, fumbled with the combination until he finally got it right, and opened the small door. Inside was a thin, plastic square, which looked like a translucent cigarette case, and a Colt .38 Special. He took out the case, which contained the diskette, flipped the computer terminal on, and inserted the software. He hit the space bar to boot the program.

"How ya doin', Doc?"

Mallory froze. He had carried that voice in his brain since the Cygnus debacle, and so recognized it instantly. He turned slowly to fix his hatred on the face. "McKay. How good of you to come."

"The pleasure's all mine, Doc," McKay said. "You know how I like hot parties. And this one looks like it's heating up pretty well." The huge M-60 was pointed directly at the physicist.

"I wouldn't fire that if I were you, McKay. I've already loaded the program throughout the system. If one bullet hits this machine, the software is designed to trigger the detonations automatically." Mallory's lips slid into a thin smile.

"Then if you touch that keyboard, I guess it won't matter if I splatter you all over the screen. The damage will already be done," McKay sneered. "So, the question is, how strong are you in the guts department?"

Mallory trembled with rage. Though he had freed his daughter and humbled the leaders of the world, he found himself once more checked by this, this *barbarian*. He eyed the revolver through the open door of the floor safe. "It looks like a standoff, then?"

"Not exactly," McKay answered. "You see, Doc, my orders read, 'dead *or* alive.' So I can just drill you now and call it a day."

"Not with that absurd cannon, you can't." It was Mallory's turn to sneer. "A burst could send a stray bullet into the computer. He picked up the detachable keyboard and held it in front of him like a shield. Then his eyes widened as he looked beyond McKay's shoulder into the doorway.

"Gentlemen, please. Such theatrics." The voice from the door carried only the slightest accent.

McKay stiffened.

"Please dispose of your weapon in a safe manner, Mr. McKay, or I will kill you where you stand."

McKay did as he was told and dropped the M-60 after first engaging the safety. Then he turned slowly, his arms raised away from his side. Looming in the doorway was a young man whose blond hair stood out in shocking contrast to his black jumpsuit. McKay knew instantly he was one of Maximov's creations. It was the arrogance that gave him away.

"Please do not touch that machine, Doctor." The tall man took a few paces into the room. "I've come to take you home. You should be glad to see me. I know Chairman Maximov will be glad to see you."

Mallory suddenly understood the full meaning of the phrase "between a rock and a hard place." He was sandwiched between these two antipodes who stood in front of him. Luck might get him past one, but two were clearly impossible. His heart sank.

Then a shot cracked, and Petrovsky grimaced, dropped to his knee, and spun, firing a long burst that fanned the doorway. McKay lunged for his M-60, but before he could get to it, another burst from the Kalashnikov laced the light machine gun and sent it spinning across the floor. The lightning movement stunned the marine.

Petrovsky slowly rose to his feet, gripping his bloody thigh just above the knee. "Get that garbage and drag it in here. I want to get a look at it." He motioned to McKay. "But first, I would be pleased if you would dispose of your side arm—very carefully."

McKay removed his Colt from its holster with his opposite hand and let it fall. Then he walked past Petrovsky, who had his rifle trained on the marine's heart, and went two paces through the door. He grabbed the freshly killed corpse by its leather-covered shoulders and dragged it into the lighted room. A small-caliber automatic pistol clattered from its hand onto the floor. He turned the body over and backed away sadly. It was Junior.

"Who is this fool?" Petrovsky gestured with his weapon.

"Just another one of your admirers," McKay answered, then turned his head away. He wasn't going to give this cruel punk any more satisfaction than he had to.

Petrovsky looked at the body for a second, then shrugged. "Now for you, Mr. McKay." He swiveled the

Kalashnikov toward his victim with one hand while he held his wound with the other.

Then an explosion boomed behind the laboratory, and the lights went out.

Petrovsky sprayed the room in a deafening barrage that emptied his clip. Then he suddenly realized his mistake, dropped his empty weapon, and lunged forward and a little to the right.

McKay gambled that the man in black would unconsciously favor the M-60 side of the room, so he dove to his left, in the opposite direction. But just as he got to his knees he felt a vicelike grip around his neck from behind. He struggled to get free from the forearm by tearing at it with his own massive hands. But it was no use. Finally he gave up and threw an elbow where he thought ribs should be. He guessed right.

Petrovsky doubled over in a knot and fought for air. A knee crashed up into his chin and snapped his head back. He spit blood and teeth and was certain his jaw was broken. In a desperate rage he lashed out into the dark with a karate kick and felt it connect.

McKay took the blow in the solar plexus and slumped to his knees, gasping. He reached for his knife as he fought for breath, then instinct told him to flatten out on the floor.

"I knew this moment would come," Petrovsky said. He drew his Makarov, pointed it at the spot where McKay's head would have been if he had been kneeling, and fired.

Still breathless, McKay lunged up and out with the Ka-Bar just as a muzzle flash split the darkness. He felt the knife slice through flesh and jam into bone. He pushed the blade deeper into what he knew was the man's groin and came up off the floor. He grabbed the hilt with his other hand and shoved up with all his strength. The two-handed heave lifted Petrovsky off the ground and pitched him, wailing in the darkness, over McKay's shoulder.

Mallory fell into the water, then regained his footing and climbed back onto the bank. He had never been so terrified in his life. The blinding flash from the machine gun against the pitch black had momentarily paralyzed him. It was a miracle he was not hit. It was also a miracle that a grenade had disabled the lab generator, causing the blackout and shutting down the computer. He had provided for sabotage by explosion, but pulling the plug simply had never occurred to him. He would have to be more careful in the future, if, indeed, he had a future.

Through a combination of luck and persistence he had been able to crawl around those two raging bulls crashing about in the dark lab. And he had made it to the door, albeit on all fours, and to safety. Now he was free of the compound and out of danger.

He had failed in his bid to secure peace and stability in the world, but he had succeeded in freeing his daughter. He might be sentenced to a lifetime of wandering the swamps alone, but at least he had accomplished that one thing for her.

What's this? He saw the outline of a boat moored just a few feet ahead in the darkness. What luck, he thought. Now he could at least get to a semblance of civilization and start all over again. He would be alive, and that, after all, would be something.

"Dr. Mallory?" came the young voice from the boat.

"Woody?" My god, it was his young savior again. "Woodrow, you don't know how glad I am to see you. What are you doing here?"

"Waiting for you."

"Another miracle. Jaysus, what a day," he panted as he crawled into the boat. "Start the motor, lad, and get us the hell out of here." Mallory waited, but nothing happened. Finally he turned toward the stern and stared into the muzzle of a .22 automatic.

"You shouldn't have let them kill Dr. Ralston," Woody said, and he pulled the trigger until the gun would no longer fire.

CHAPTER
TWENTY-ONE ——————————

The bottle-nosed C-130 angled off toward the northeast, its running lights blinking red and green against the night sky. McKay stretched out on the front deck of Mobile One, which did its best to take up all of the cargo bay in the giant Hercules. The rest of the Guardians were packed on or around the wide machine.

Except for Casey. He lay on a bunk rigged up aft while a white-coated physician, a specialist in gunshot wounds, tended his garbaged shoulder, along with a nurse who had made the trip down from Washington. Tom occasionally would hover over them like a mother hen, making sure all their education didn't lead them to do something stupid.

"How's the kid?" McKay asked when he saw Tom pass him on a trip back from the rear of the aircraft.

"He's holding his own," Tom said. "They've pumped six units of blood into him and got him stable. The doctor's looking at his shoulder now from the standpoint of reconstruction. The preliminary verdict is that Casey won't be pitching in the majors, but he can fly unhindered all he wants."

McKay was relieved. He may have given Casey more than a full ration of shit over the past two years, but he still loved the kid and couldn't imagine a mission without him.

He was glad that the others had come through without a scratch, except for him. His neck hurt and his solar plexus was still a little tender, but his condition was minor compared to the kid's.

He wondered about the warrior of Maximov's he had killed back at the compound. The young man couldn't have been over twenty-five, yet there was something about him that had made him appear older. Something snakey in the eyes. McKay shuddered. Well, at least that was over.

Now he had to figure out what he was going to tell the President. MacGregor would not be pleased to hear that Mallory had escaped—again. *Damn!* McKay thought. The wily son of a bitch must have sneaked out while he was putting the quietus on that young gladiator. Then the physicist had simply disappeared. Vanished! He would just have to tell the President that there were priorities, even in this business. And survival was at the top of the list.

McKay was more than a little curious about Woody. He, too, had vanished along with the boat, and McKay wondered if there was some connection. Regardless, he hoped the boy was safe. He had even thought about bringing him back to Washington with him. He could have been like a mascot for the Guardians. And instead of having no parents, he suddenly could have had four fathers. Well, three fathers and an older brother, considering Casey's maturity level. But, it was just as well. Woody probably couldn't handle having four fathers, especially ones as crazy as the Guardians.

How would he explain Mallory's disappearance? McKay

kept coming back to the question. After thinking himself into several dead ends, he finally threw up his hands and said, "Fuck Mallory. Let the goddamn snakes get him."

Everyone in the plane turned and looked at him.

EPILOGUE

Woody paddled silently up the murky slough. He had traveled all night, using the frog light, and had made it almost to the mouth of the White by dawn—well, at least to the canal that joined the Arkansas to the White and then flowed on to the Mississippi.

He had dumped the doctor's body just before sunup. He was tired of looking at it anyway as the light passed over it in the night—with its eyes and mouth wide open like that, just gaping. He had had to do it, of course. After all, the Ralstons had been good to him, so he had squared it with them the best he knew how.

He had gone through the locks of the canal and up the Arkansas after first light. He didn't know how far he'd come in miles, but it was a long way, and he was tired. That's why he had turned up into the slough. He would get well away from the barge traffic on the river and tie up. Then he would sleep until dark.

He paddled around a tight bend, and abruptly an old river lake appeared at the head of the slough. This would make a good spot. He was also hungry, so he might as well catch some crappie and have a bite. These old cypress lakes were the best for that kind of fishing.

He moved the big john boat into the lake and immediately saw something strange at its middle. There, sticking out of the water, was some sort of metal arm with a kind of finger on it. He could tell the thing hadn't been there very long because it was still pretty shiny and new-looking. He got closer to it, this monolithic object so out of place against the almost prehistoric look of the cypress-kneed lake. He paddled right up to it and saw some writing on its side. Some letters were covered over, so Woody reached out and wiped away the mud that obscured them. Then he read the words. He scratched his head and read again, then wondered what "CYGNUS X-1 FEL LASER" meant.